THE
FIRST
COURSE

THE FIRST COURSE

THE RESTAURANT DIARIES

BRANDON D. BRADLEY

Bradley Group Publishing
McDonough, GA

THE FIRST COURSE

This book is based on true events. The author has tried to recreate events, locales, and conversations from memory. To maintain anonymity, the author has changed the names of individuals and places. Some events have been slightly altered for entertainment, and some dialogue has been recreated.

THE FIRST COURSE copyright 2022 Branddon D. Bradley

Paperback ISBN: 978-1-7332237-1-3

Published by Bradley Group Publishing
McDonough, GA

Printed in the United States of America

First Edition, June 2022

Cover Design by Make Your Mark Publishing Solutions
Interior Layout by Make Your Mark Publishing Solutions
Editing by Make Your Mark Publishing Solutions

*To my mom and my dad, for without you there would be no me.
Thank you for your guidance, understanding, and mostly, your love.*

To Don and Brian, the best big brothers anyone could have.

*And of course, my wife, Carmen, and my four
wonderful children and grandchild, Caiden.*

I love you all.

Acknowledgements

This book is based on my many years in the restaurant industry and the beginning of my management career. Thank you to all my former managers and coworkers that helped form the manager I became. All your leadership and guidance will be forever remembered.

Thank you, T. Reeves Photography LLC for the wonderful photos for my first and second book. Thank you, Monique Mensah and Make your Mark Publishing Solutions for staying on me and making me a better writer.

Thanks to my Wife and my mom for always believing in me!

Thank you, the readers, for supporting Restaurant Diaries and also making me a better writer with any comments and suggestions that you may have.

CARTER

Hello, everyone! It is your boy, Carter, and welcome back to the continuation of the Restaurant Diaries saga! So, you already learned if you read the first book, *A la Carte*, that I have been in the restaurant industry since I was fourteen years old and working at the Blue Crab for the last seven years at this point.

I've seen everything in the restaurant industry from guns being drawn on workers, to attempted robberies, to knives being pulled, and to drugs being sold. After all these trials and errors, I honestly believe I have mastered the art of being a true restaurateur. In these seven years working with the Blue Crab, I had no idea I was going to become a manager, but now it was time to embark on that journey.

From working with bosses like Big Shirley (who was the meanest manager ever), B.T. (the most unprofessional manager ever), and others, I knew that—at the very least—I could run a restaurant as good as they could. Working with all these different personalities, I'd seen everything that can be seen working at a restaurant. I knew everything that falls under what *not* to do. Becoming a manager was a no brainer!

Don't drop ice cream on the floor and still serve it to the customer. Check.

Don't spit in your customers' food. Check.

Don't give your employees alcoholic beverages during their shift. Check.

Don't chase customers down the street. Check.

After all these unbelievable experiences, I was ready for this promotion and management role. I was going to show everyone how it's done. This management thing would be a cakewalk. So I thought!

ᴮE A LEADER

I couldn't believe it! I was no longer a server, but a freshly appointed manager. I was excited and nervous at the same time. Excited about the new venture but nervous because this was completely new to me. Chris, my area director, told me that I was going to another location to do my CIT (Crabmaster in Training) training. I wanted to stay at my current location but was advised they never let you train where you are currently an hourly worker. Looking back on it, I was glad that I didn't stay there. It would've been difficult to train at a location where you were friends with everyone.

I had never been to this other location before, but I was looking forward to the challenge. The training consisted of an eight-week training program in which you would work every position in the restaurant. Being a server was easy, but working every position was going to be a challenge. I was now going to have interactions with everyone, from the cooks to the customers!

My days would start off with my training general manager, A.J. He was the first person I met when I came to the building. As I approached the building, he was already standing at the front door, waving and smiling. It set me at ease because I was nervous with anticipation. A.J. was a tall and slender older man. He had the build of an ex-athlete that still kept himself active. You could tell immediately that he was a kind man, but he carried himself in a way that told you he was important. He was waiting for me with my CIT folder.

"You must be Carter! I heard great things about you, young man! Are you ready to be a leader?" he asked.

"Yes, I am ready to be a leader!"

As A.J. walked me around and introduced me to people, I felt important just being in his presence. After he engaged in conversation with other workers, he would look at them and say, "Be a leader!"

I asked him, "Do you say *be a leader* to everyone here?"

He stated, "Yes I do, young man. See, I expect everyone that I work with to be a leader. If we are a restaurant full of leaders, all with a leadership mindset, we will achieve massive results."

I was already looking forward to working with him. A.J. made a pot of fresh coffee and would go around and serve his crew. He would engage with everyone and ask how they were doing. There was never a day that I saw him that he would not say, "Be a leader!" I was hugely impressed with him and his position.

A.J. always left early on the days he opened the restaurant. He advised me that he left every day to go to his executive office. In all my time at the Blue Crab, I had worked for six different general managers. None of these general managers had an executive office. This was highly impressive, and I made sure to hang on every word he said. Surely, one day I could have an executive office as well.

As I was dreaming about this day, he must've picked up on that, because he said, "Young man, on your last week of training I will take you to my executive office and show you around." I was elated and looking forward to the day I would get to go there. I was honored to be working with such an important person and even more honored that he invited me to his prestigious executive office.

I had so many questions in my head regarding this office. *Why is he the only GM to get an executive office? Where is it located? I wonder if it's in a large skyscraper building. Do we have to take an elevator up to the top floor to get there?*

A.J. looked at me and said, "Carter, please do not talk to anyone else about my executive office because I don't allow everyone to come." I felt proud and privileged that he was giving me an invite. I would not let A.J. down! I looked admirably at A.J. and said, "Sir, my lips are sealed!"

I worked with A.J. often my first two weeks. We would come in early before the crew and check the condition of the restaurant from the prior night. He would have me take temperatures of all the coolers and log all our food adherences. A.J. also would have me check on the kitchen crew every day as well. I would check for attendance and uniform standard, and set the expectation for productivity.

The crew didn't care for the CITs that much. A.J.'s store was a training store and they were used to getting training managers every other month. They didn't like the fact they were training the manager trainees while these trainees were expected to monitor and coach them on productivity. To be honest, I understood where they were coming from. I knew nothing about the kitchen, apart from the few times that I would come in and attempt to fry food with the cooks at my previous restaurant. We were taught to act like a manager (be a leader) from the first day of training. So, you were getting trained by the crew, but if they were late, unproductive, or used profanity, we had to chastise them. They hated us for this. Although I understood where they were coming from, I knew that I was there to do a job. I would never stop short of telling them what they needed to do.

Looking back on it, someone should've slapped me upside the head. I wasn't humble enough to learn from these people who were mostly older than me. I thought I was better than them because I was a manager. I couldn't have been so wrong! I had a lot to learn!

I was into my second week of training when Chris came in to visit A.J.'s restaurant. He was overseeing fifteen different Blue Crabs, so you would only see him about twice a month. However, he would be in contact with all his restaurants daily. I went up to say hello to Chris and to again thank him for getting me into the management program. As I was walking toward him, Chris was frowning with his arms crossed and a look of irritation on his face. I reluctantly said hello to him. Instead of saying hello back to me, he just looked at me and said, "What happened to your shirt?"

"Um, what do you mean?" I questioned.

He stated, "Why is your shirt so wrinkled? Did you even bother ironing your shirt?"

I looked down at my shirt—it was severely wrinkled. I was astonished because I did iron it before I came into work. As I thought about it, I explained to Chris that I did iron my shirt, but it was very hot this morning and my sweat made my shirt stick to me a little bit. I also explained that my seatbelt had bunched up my shirt. Chris wasn't buying my excuses.

He stated, "If you are going to be a manager for me, your attire will never look this bad again. You have to be a professional, and professionals don't dress like this!"

Now I was agitated that this man was talking to me in this tone!

"Do you not think it was hot for me today? I also drove to work and had a seatbelt on. Do you see me wrinkled and looking unprofessional?"

I apologized and said that it wouldn't happen again.

"I know this won't happen again! I will not allow it. Come to think about it, I will not allow you to work looking like this today. You need to go home and change your attire and then return to work. Do you understand?"

I told him that I understood. I was surprised by his actions, but I left immediately. I was angry with him and thought he was doing too much. As I was leaving, I saw the look on A.J.'s face. He seemed disappointed.

I got into the car and was fuming. *How dare Chris talk to me in this manner and in front of team members!* I put my car into gear and screeched out the parking lot. *He wants me to go and get another shirt, huh? How about I get no shirt and just go back home. I could get another job*, I thought. I was not going to be abused by Chris or any manager. To hell with the Blue Crab.

On my way home, I stopped by my favorite pizza place and got me a small pizza and a drink. I was going to eat my pizza, take a nap, and then find me a new job. A job that wasn't going to have the boss try to degrade me in front of people.

I got home and saw that my answering machine was beeping. I clicked the button and listened to the message. It was A.J.

"Hello, Carter! Please give me a call when you get this message."

I quickly deleted the message and went to eat my pizza. My phone rang a couple more times, and I could tell on my caller ID that it was the Blue Crab. I felt a little guilty for not answering, so when it rang again, this time I answered. It was A.J.

"Hey, Carter, you've been gone for a while. Are you coming back?"

I hesitated and said, "I'm not sure!"

"I saw your anger when you left the restaurant. I knew you were upset, but I never thought that you would not return. I pegged you to be a leader, and I believe in you."

I now felt ashamed. Although I had just met A.J., I did not want to let him down. The fact that he believed in me meant something. I started thinking about one day being in his shoes. I wanted to impact lives and have people look up to me. I also wanted to have an executive office like him one day.

"Is it too late for me to come back?" I asked. "I've been gone for a while and I know Chris is probably upset with me."

"Carter, you just come back to the restaurant and let me deal with Chris. Are you ready to be a leader?"

"Yes, I am ready to be a leader," I replied.

"Well then, iron your shirt and get back to the restaurant!"

Wow, how did A.J. do this? I was just ready to throw in the towel, but one short conversation with him had me pumped up and ready to go. I put my pizza in the fridge, ironed my shirt, and made my way back to the restaurant.

As I pulled back into the parking lot of the Blue Crab, there was A.J. waiting for me at the door, waving and looking excited to see me, just like my first day when I met him. I felt embarrassed for giving up so easy. I thought to myself that I would never disappoint him again. I walked up to A.J., shook his hand firmly, and then saluted him. I shouted, "One leader reporting for duty, sir."

A.J. just smiled and walked me back into the building.

The Inmates (Workers) Are Running the Prison

I knew in the first week of training that I wasn't a kitchen person. The company started you off working in the prep area and then on the cook line. I hated both positions, especially prep. Standing in one spot prepping food for hours was boring and too monotonous for me. My back and legs were cramping after the first day. The cook line was a little bit better. At least you got to move around a little. However, after doing two days straight of frying, I thought I was going to have carpal tunnel from lifting the fry baskets countless times over an eight-hour period. I even had the fry basket handle imprint on my hand once the shift ended.

The next place they had me work was on the grill. I was petrified with the grill. I had never worked the grill a day in my life at home or at work. I also wasn't looking forward to working with the grill cooks. They were prima donnas! For whatever reason, the cooks at the Blue Crab always thought they were running things and the managers always let them get away with it. They would yell at servers, cuss at them, or just ignore them altogether. Servers would oftentimes go and get a manager on them, but rarely was anything done about it. The managers would usually console the cooks or try to reason with them. I would come to find out later that most managers can't handle coming up to the line to cook. They would rather deal with a confrontational cook then send them home and cook themselves.

This location had a cook that I think hated life in general. I will never forget this piece of crap. His name was Terry. Terry was tall and lanky with long messy hair and an equally long and messy beard. Management never required him to wear a beard restraint, which was weird to me. They always made sure the other cooks had them on, but not Terry. We always got complaints about hair in the food when he was the grill cook. Even with all the complaints, the managers would never say anything to him.

God forbid if a server had the audacity to ask how long their food was going to be. He would stop all cooking just to address the server.

"Hey, ass wipe, the food will be ready when it's ready. Now stop asking me about the food unless you going to come back here and cook it yourself."

Terry had no problem serving food that was burned and dared you to return the food. If any food came back to the kitchen, he would be sure to take extra long recooking the item. Even if management came and asked about the food, he would just ignore them.

When I worked on the cook line with him for my two fry shifts, he was not helpful at all. He loved giving the servers a hard time, but also giving his fellow line cooks a hard time. Most of the other cooks couldn't keep up with his speed and demands and he would yell at them to keep up the pace. Oftentimes, he would just push them out the way and do it himself if he thought they were too slow. You could tell he thought he was better than everyone else. I hated even being around this dude. I had to be cautious and remember that I was only here for training.

"Hey, you need to move faster and get the hell out my way," he barked. I completely ignored him. He surely was not talking to me, I thought. I must have angered him because he barked louder, "Yo! I said you need to get the hell out of my way or move faster."

Out of sheer instinct, I barked back at him, "Yo, motha"—I had to stop myself from cursing at him—"you may want to rethink talking to me like you are out of your mind." He just stared at me like he wanted to punch me. I stared at him back. I wasn't too far into this management thing if I had to lose it. I was not about to let this dude punk me out. Part of me wanted him to swing on me. He got the picture, turned around, and went back to work. He wouldn't speak to me for the remainder of the shift, and I was cool with that.

Terry and I ended up getting into another confrontation at the end of my second shift working on the line. My manager, Amy, was teaching me how to count food. We had to count all unused prepped food at the end of the night to gauge what we were going to prep the next day. As we were counting food, I guess Terry was ready to go because he started cleaning his floors. While Amy and I were counting food, this guy decided to spray the water hose everywhere. He was literally spraying the bottoms of our pant legs and our ankles with water.

Amy sighed under her breath and said, "He is such a jerk. He sprays the managers every night. We should probably just get out of his way. We can come back and count when he is finished." I was in awe that the managers were being such pushovers around this guy.

I yelled, "Hey, you need to stop spraying us with the water hose!"

He yelled back, "Get out of the way and you won't get sprayed!"

He went back to spraying us. I had to step up to him. I was technically not a full-blown manager yet, but I acted like it at this point. I had to because the manager was just going to let it happen.

Although I had no authority, I looked him dead in the eye and told him, "Dude, if you spray us one more time with that water, I will be firing you on the spot!" Now, I am not sure if he believed what my mouth was saying or what my eyes were saying. My eyes were saying, *If you spray me one more time, I'm going to beat the life out of you.* He must have read my eyes, because he put the water hose down and pouted off to do something else.

This would not be the only employee that I had to chastise. I had a prep girl, Malinda, who was always late. She was at least thirty minutes late for every shift that she worked. All the other kitchen people complained about her every day. They were upset that she could work here with her constant horrible attendance. On top of that, her productivity was horrible. She would come in late, clock in, and then spend fifteen minutes in the restroom before she would even start.

I ended up confronting her about this. I waited for her to come out of the restroom where none of her coworkers would be around.

"Malinda, can I talk to you for a quick sec?" I asked when she came out.

She said, "Sure, what's up!" She had no worries because no one ever said anything to her about her lack of productivity or attendance.

I started off saying, "Look, Malinda, no one wants to say anything to you, but being late to all of your shifts can't be tolerated. Not only are you late, but you get clocked in and spend another fifteen minutes in the bathroom before you get started."

Malinda stood there with her arms crossed, with an irritated smirk on her face.

I continued, "Moving forward, you have to start being on time for work. You also need to be ready for work when you get in. No more getting clocked in and then spending another fifteen minutes in the bathroom."

She still stood there with a smirk on her face.

I ended by saying, "Do you understand that we expect your adherence to these standards?"

She barked, "What I don't understand is how you have the audacity to tell me anything. You are not a manager; you are a trainee!"

"Just try me again," I told her, "and I will personally write you up the next time that you are late. You can count on this."

Malinda stormed off and went and got our soft-ass manager Amy. Amy stated, "Carter, Malinda has been here for a long time and we have no issues with her.

I will handle it!" Who was Amy kidding? I knew that nothing would ever be done about it.

The next day, however, she was on time for her shift, but she would never talk to me for the rest of my training. No love lost with me! At the end of her shift, I observed her washing her hair in the prep sink. I was about to say something to her, but Amy walked past her and did not say a word. *Yuck, why would she be washing her hair in the sinks where we prep food at?* I shrugged and walked past Malinda as well. If management didn't care, neither did I.

* * *

We had another young lady there that I had a huge disdain for. Her name was Jessie. She was a server who was defiant about everything. She had multiple piercings, which never bothered me, but the Blue Crab policy is that all front of the house employees are to not have any facial piercings besides ear piercings. And you could have no more than two ear piercings. I guess this rule didn't apply to Jessie because she had piercings on her eyebrow, multiple piercings on both ears, a lip piercing, and a nose piercing. Her nose piercing bothered me because she was always playing with it. *Yikes, germs, snot, and boogers,* was all I could think of when I saw her!

Jessie always got into confrontations with other servers, and the guests didn't like her that much as well. She hated the CIT trainees. She would voice her opinion about us all the time and she wasn't shy about it. She would tell the managers with trainees in the same vicinity, "I'll do what a manager says, but not no damn trainee." The managers always laughed at her but avoided any confrontation.

Jessie was known for not completing any of her side work or detailing her section before she left for the day. All servers had to do side work to keep the restaurant flowing. Silverware had to be rolled, salad dressings and other condiments had to be filled, tea and lemonade had to be made. Every server had something assigned to them, including Jessie, but she was the only server who couldn't care less. Other servers who came behind her in a section often complained about having to manicure the section before they could ever get a table. After her tables left, she would not wipe them or clean the floors. Once her customers were done, so was she.

One day, the managers had me checking out the servers before they left. No one gave me a hard time about detailing their area except for Jessie. I pointed out the things that needed to be done, but she brushed me off. She said, "I did a good enough job cleaning the area. I'm not about to do anything else, except go home." I told her that she could not leave without cleaning her section. She just walked away from me and went and sat down in the lobby.

I followed her and said, "I really need you to complete your area."

"Maaan, I am not doing anything else. Would you just leave me alone? I am waiting on my ride to get here and then I am leaving," she yelled. I was upset and went and got the acting manager.

Fortunately, soft Amy was not working and I went and got Amanda, another manager. Amanda was the manager who was second in charge when A.J. wasn't in the building. Since A.J. was always at his executive office, Amanda was always at the restaurant. No one gave Amanda any issues. She was stern and knew everything about the restaurant. The word was A.J. was grooming her to be a general manager one day. Amanda sat down with the both of us and heard both of our sides. After hearing what I had to say, Amanda looked at Jessie and asked, "Jessie, did you refuse to do what Carter asked you to do.?"

Jessie looked her dead in the eye and said, "*Yep.*"

Wow! She admitted to it and couldn't care less. I knew that she was going to get in trouble for refusing an order. I was patiently waiting to hear Amanda's response and for her to put Jessie into place. Amanda simply sighed and stated, "You two must find a way to get along with each other." I was waiting on more from Amanda, but that was it.

I was shocked, angry, and in total disbelief that Jessie was not getting reprimanded for her actions. This rude girl looked at Amanda and said, "I will never do what he asks me to do. If you have a problem with it, then talk to A.J." She got up and walked away. Amanda did nothing. I wanted to yank Jessie up by her nose ring and throw her out the building.

I decided at that moment that I was done saying anything to this crew because the managers were never going to hold them accountable. I was going to put my head down, bite my tongue, and finish my training without a word. It was made clear—the workers were running this place!

THE BIG WIGS

A.J.'s restaurant was not only a training restaurant (hard to believe), but they also would hold regional training, certification testing, and general manager meetings there. A.J. would often refer to his restaurant as the model restaurant. It was a model restaurant only when he was there. Because he spent the other half of his day at the executive office, the restaurant was a disaster when he was not present.

I knew that I was at the place to be—training at this restaurant. I really wanted to stay at this location when my training was up. Although I did not care for the crew so much, I knew working for A.J. would get me places. I also thought I could help the restaurant not be a disaster when he wasn't available.

Chris would hold his general manager meetings at A.J.'s restaurant every month. I happened to be working there for one of the meetings. I made sure I was dressed particularly nice on these days. The general managers were the Big Wigs and I wanted to make sure that I impressed them.

A.J. would give me the keys to the building any time that I opened with him. The restaurant stayed locked until we opened at 11:00 a.m. I oversaw letting anyone into the building prior to opening. This included all employees, vendors, contractors, and managers. So, when the general manager meetings were being held, I had to let all the general managers into the building as well as Chris (the director). A.J. would tell me to shine and be a leader! I felt so honored and privileged. I had only met a few of the GMs before, but that day I would meet them all and I couldn't wait.

As I opened the door repeatedly, I tried my best to stand out. I introduced myself as the new CIT. Some of them acknowledged me and held mild chitchat and others just nodded and kept walking. Although I was crossing my fingers that I would stay at A.J.'s restaurant, I really had no idea where I would end up. So, one of these people that I was opening the door for was going to be my future boss.

I remember the first general manager that came to the meeting was a hyper lady. As soon as I opened the door, she said, "Hey, love! You must be the CIT!" She had way too much energy for 8:00 a.m. She introduced herself as Jackson. I had never met a woman named Jackson before! I remembered thinking that Jackson needed to lay off the caffeine.

The next person that came was a tall Fine Sister named Lisa. I remembered meeting her before when I did my server certification a couple of years previously. The Blue Crab had all the trainers meet at a hotel's conference room. We had a full day of training by this lady. I didn't know that she was a general manager at the time. I thought she was a corporate trainer. She held herself with so much esteem and confidence. She was highly impressive and articulate. She had poise and took charge of the meeting.

All the guys there were salivating over her, including myself. The girls at the meeting were shaking their heads at us, but they had to admit that she was beautiful. I had a small crush on her instantly, even though I knew she was waaaaayyyy out of my league.

I had forgot about Lisa and my crush until I opened the door and saw her. Instantly, my crush was back. I think I blushed, but she was all business. She said hello to me and kept it moving. I was simply happy that she said hello.

As the other general managers came in, I opened the door for them as well. I had not met any of the others before. They were mostly women, apart from my former GM, Sal, and my present GM, A.J. I thought every general manager was in, but fifteen minutes after the meeting had already started, the back door rang.

I hurried to the door, thinking that it must be a late delivery coming in. When I looked out the window, I was shocked to see who was standing there. It was worse than a late delivery. It was B.T. I had not seen B.T. since my first year at the Blue Crab. B.T. was the most unprofessional manager I had ever met before. I worked for her in my first year as an employee with the Blue Crab. That was almost seven years ago. I wondered what she was doing standing there. I instantly had flashbacks of her making me drink a Long Island iced tea and a shot when I used to work with her in my beginning stages of the Blue Crab.

I thought to myself that there was no possible way she was a general manager. As I stood there in shock, still looking out the window, she looked at me and stated, "Are you going to just stand there or open the door?" Hesitantly, I opened the door. She walked in and didn't say hello or anything. She walked right passed me as if I didn't exist.

I shouted out, "Hello, Kassaundra!" I was surprised I even remembered her first name. I barely spoke to her in the past and we all called her B.T. (Big Titties) behind her back anyway. She never stopped walking and never acknowledged me either as she walked to where the meeting was going on for the general managers. I was shocked that Chris had promoted her. From what I remember, she was unprofessional, rude, anti-social, and borderline angry! How was she a general manager?

I did not realize their meeting would last the entire day. I oversaw keeping their drinks refilled and making sure they ordered lunch. Every time I brought them something, Jackson would comment, "Thanks, love." I continued to check on them as often as I could but was sure not to bring the coffee pot around to Jackson. I also tried my best to stay away from B.T.

A.J. ended up coming to the kitchen where I was at. He told me that I didn't need to keep coming back there checking on them. I got the point, stayed away, and focused on the restaurant.

A few times, the general managers except B.T. would come into the kitchen to get coffee or soft drinks on their breaks. B.T. would go outside on her break and smoke cigarettes. Surprisingly, all the employees were on their best behavior with the Big Wigs in the building. Come to think about it, the terrible people were conveniently off work that day. No Terry, Jessie, or Malinda. I never asked, but I'm sure A.J. didn't want those troublemakers there while the Big Wigs were in the building. Very smart man!

On one of their breaks, A.J. was in the kitchen with a few of them. It was around 3:00 p.m. and a couple of the general managers joked toward A.J. that it was a little late for him to be at the restaurant. The GM Jackson said, "Love, don't you still have to go to your executive office?" A.J. answered with pride and said, "Absolutely, I never miss a day!" I remembered thinking they were haters. They were all jealous they didn't have an executive office. I admired A.J. for his dedication!

As they were all leaving, I made sure that I shook hands and said goodbye to all of them. Jackson said, "Goodbye, love" and gave me a hug. Sal and I chit-chatted for a little while as he asked how everything was going. He was sure to tell me to "Keep up the good work and don't let me down!" I just held my tongue. I guess he really thought he was the one that made this promotion happen for me. He was acting as if he was my biggest advocate. This was the first time that I recalled playing the political games. I went along, letting him think he was the reason for my promotion, although I was the one who pursued Chris about me going into management, not Sal.

As we were saying goodbye, Sal attempted to introduce me to the angry and anti-social B.T. She cut him off midway through his introduction. "I already know Carter," she said. "I'm surprised he's still around. The last time I saw him, he was crying like a little girl because some little girl dumped him." I instantly remembered how much I hated her. "Now he is about to be a manager. Let me see, have you grown some hair on your chest yet?" She motioned toward me like she was going to peek inside my shirt.

I backed away swiftly and just stared at her. As I began walking away, I heard Sal and B.T. laughing. I still didn't like this woman at all. I wondered how she became a general manager. It couldn't have been due to her personality! I hoped to never work for this lady.

Afterward, Sal formally introduced me to Lisa. I was fumbling over my words because I was nervous speaking to her. She seemed no-nonsense and profoundly serious. She was a tad bit intimidating, but still beautiful. I was hoping Lisa would give me a hug like Jackson did. She just shook my hand and walked off.

After Sal introduced me to everyone, he left, and I went back to working. A.J. came up to me with his jacket on and said that he was going to get some gas and head to the office. He told me

I could finish up with my paperwork and leave when I was done. I thanked him but felt sorry for him that he had to still go to the office. He must have been getting the big bucks. Although an executive office was intriguing, I wasn't sure if I wanted his responsibilities.

Let's Party

Even though this was a training restaurant, they knew how to have fun. I noticed when I worked the evening shifts that the crew would always go out to party after work. Some of the crew would ask me to go out, but I would always decline.

My first day in training, A.J. went over—in detail—about not fraternizing with the crew. I was careful to not do this. The last thing that I wanted was to get fired during training. This one server, Carrie, had a small crush on me. She was the first server to introduce herself to me when I came to this location. Every day that I would open the restaurant, she would come in and bring me a fresh cup of coffee. She had a heart drawn onto the coffee cup. Within my first week, she asked me if I had a girlfriend. When I told her that I did not, she blushed and walked away. She was the one that repeatedly asked me to go out. I was incredibly careful on not giving in. I heard that a lot of the parties would start at the bar but end up at someone's home. I did not need this kind of problem.

I couldn't hang out with the crew, but I could hang out with the managers. One evening when I was training on how to properly close the restaurant, Amanda (one of the managers) asked me to go to the local bar and have a drink with her. I told her that I would. After we were finished with everything and locked up the building, she told me to follow her in her car.

I didn't realize that the bar was literally right around the corner. It was a little hole in the wall bar, but it looked clean and safe. Once we got into the parking lot, I jumped out and walked into the bar with her. As soon as I walked into the bar, I saw several of the employees from the Blue Crab. They saw me and Amanda as well. They didn't seem surprised to see her but did a double take when they saw me. I figured out quickly this wasn't Amanda's first time at this bar with the crew.

At first, I felt like I was sabotaged. Carrie was there and as soon as she saw me, she jumped up and came running up to me. She gave me a long, seductive hug. She had her body pressed on me tight. I had to physically pull her off me. She invited us to sit down at their table and have a drink. Amanda declined their offer and said that we were going to sit at the bar. Carrie looked disappointed.

As soon as I sat down at the bar, I addressed the fact that I felt uncomfortable being here. I told her this did not seem like it was her first time coming in here when the crew was here. She told me, "If you feel uncomfortable, then you should leave." She didn't have to tell me twice. I jumped up to leave and Amanda grabbed my arm. She said, "Carter, before you leave, let me ask you a question." I said sure. Amanda said, "Did you know the crew was going to be here?"

I said "No" as I continued to walk to the exit.

She hurried after me as I put my hand on the door to leave. "Carter, did we sit at the table and join the crew for drinks?"

I said, "No."

Finally, she said, "Then relax, dude, you are fine. You can't get in any trouble for fraternization because you didn't willingly go to a function that you knew the crew would be at. You also didn't associate with them when you found out they were there. Just relax, have a drink with me, and then if you still want to go, then go."

I obliged and had a drink that turned into a couple of drinks, but I knew Amanda was full of it. She was bending the rules to make sure that we couldn't *technically* get fired.

Although we didn't sit at a table with the crew, the crew came and sat at the bar with us. Of course, Carrie found a way to sit right next to me. I ended up staying at the bar for about an hour. It was a pretty cool little bar, with good burgers and drinks as well as karaoke. As I was about to go, some of the crew begged me to stay, but I knew better than that. Like I said, most of these parties ended up at someone's house. I hurried up and got out of there.

As I got to the parking lot, Carrie came running up to me. "Carter, why don't you stay?" she asked. I told her that it was late, and I needed to get home. "Well, I hate to see you leave," she stated as she stared into my eyes. She came up to me like she was going to attempt a kiss. I turned around and got into my car. I didn't want these kinds of problems. She seemed disappointed, but I couldn't care less.

As the weeks went on, I found myself going to this bar often, although I knew this was not smart. I'd figure, I wouldn't get caught. And as long as I didn't go to one of these after bar closing parties I should be safe. Surely there would be some times, people from work wouldn't be there. Besides, It was cool to have a place so close to unwind after work. Unfortunately, there was never a time that I went there and didn't run into someone from the Blue Crab. Although this was a deterrence, there were also a lot of women there who didn't work at the Blue Crab. Of course,

Carrie was there every time and tried to act like she was my girl-friend. In her eyes, I think she was happy that she was spending time with me.

Believe it or not, all the managers came to this bar as well, except for A.J. I guess the fraternization rule was not in effect at this location. It was definitely not the *model restaurant*. He couldn't have known what was going on with his staff and managers.

I was still young at the time, so partying was right up my al-ley. We would dance and sing karaoke almost every time that we were there. I started having so much fun that I even invited some of my old coworkers from my old Blue Crab to come hang out with us. They came out and had a great time. However, one of my old coworkers pulled me to the side and advised me to be careful because I could be fired if Chris found out. He told me this was not normal for the managers to hang out with the crew like this.

I had to be honest—this didn't seem quite normal. This was the fourth Blue Crab that I worked at, and I had never seen such a blatant view of fraternization like at this location. Most of the managers in the past were much more discreet with their indis-cretions than at this location. I wish I would've taken my friend's advice and left the partying alone, but I didn't. I knew it was not worth it to get fired for partying with the crew, but once again, I figured I wouldn't get caught. This was just the training store. I could party with them, but I told myself that I would not party with my crew once they sent me to my permanent location.

Despite partying and having fun, the crew used this place as an opportunity to talk bad about the managers. Of course, they wouldn't talk about the manager that currently was there at the time. The crew would often tell me that I didn't have to do certain things. They told me that the managers never did what they were teaching me to do. The managers would also start to unwind and after a couple of drinks they would complain about A.J. and him leaving early each day. *Here we go again, talking about A.J.*

One night, we were having such a good time at the bar, the talk began about moving the party to one of their homes. This was my biggest fear. It was already enough that I was going to the bar, but going to someone's house was another thing. Amanda begged me to go. "Stop being such a nerd and come hang out. Nothing is going to happen."

Carrie was right behind her also pleading with me to go. "C'mon, Carter, it will be fun." Reluctantly, I obliged and went.

About twenty people came to the house including myself. The party was uneventful. We were just drinking and telling dumb stories about what happened at work that day. Carrie kept pulling on me to come to the other room, but I knew better than this. After a few failed attempts, she seemed annoyed. She got the picture and left. I was relieved! I didn't want to make a mistake. The last thing that I wanted to do was get intoxicated and end up sleeping with this girl.

After about an hour, people started to leave. The party had dwindled down to about six of us.

It was obvious the party was over, and I was getting ready to leave as others were also leaving. As we were about to walk out, we heard a strange noise upstairs. The guy that was holding the party looked at all of us and yelled, "Do you guys know who the hell is upstairs?" In unison, we all shrugged. He had blocked off the upstairs part of his home so people wouldn't go up there. Besides, he had thought it was just the six of us left.

Now seeming to be embarrassed and worried, the guy stated, "Hey guys, don't leave yet. I don't know who is upstairs! I shouldn't have let everyone from the bar come over. I know you Blue Crab people but I didn't know everyone else."

Who invites people over they don't know? I thought. *Yes, he should be worried.*

He grabbed a baseball bat and proceeded up the stairs, gesturing for us to come with him. The rest of us followed him. He paused when he got to the top of the stairs. It was silent. We all stood there for about twenty seconds until we heard a sound again. It sounded like moans! It was coming from one of his bedrooms. He started walking slowly toward the room with the bat held high. We all followed behind him. With each step, I just knew my management career was going to be over.

As we got closer to the room, the moans got louder. We thought someone was in this room having sex! He nudged the door open slightly. As he peered in, someone was sitting at his computer desk. Instantly, we all knew who it was. It was Carrie! I thought she had left. We stood in shock looking at her as she had no idea we were even standing there.

Carrie was slouched back in a chair with one leg perched on a desk. There was a porno video on the computer screen. She was completely naked and masturbating. She was so into it, with her eyes closed. At this point, she was moaning so loud that she didn't hear anyone standing there. As the door swung open more, the light from the hallway crept into the room. This jolted her from her trance. With her fingers still inserted, she turned to look at the door and saw everyone standing there.

She was so shocked, embarrassed, and drunk that she grabbed her clothes and ran out of the house butt naked. She forgot to grab her shoes, she was in such a hurry. We laughed for about ten minutes straight. The guy that was holding the party was the only one not humored. He was disgusted that she was doing that in his home. As we kept laughing, he told all of us to get out. Everyone left the house, but we were joking hysterically as we walked out. Amanda looked at me and said, "I guess you should've gone with her to the other room. That could've been you instead of the porno video!"

This incident was the talk of the day at work the next day. I was nervous, but no one mentioned that Amanda or I attended the party. Carrie was scheduled to work that evening. I think everyone from the day shift stayed to see if she was going to come in. I didn't think that she was going to appear unless she was so drunk that she didn't remember it. To everyone's disappointment, she did not show up. We were never going to see her again, but the memory would last forever!

—Executive Office

A.J. always made sure to ask me how things had gone on my prior shift. I lied and said everything was great. The team and the managers acted differently when he was working. When he was in the building, everyone was great. The issue was, he was barely ever at work. He would always open the restaurant and then would go to the executive office halfway through his shift.

I remembered thinking this was unfair to him. The company had him splitting time between the restaurant and the executive office. Most of his managers worked ten-hour shifts. A.J. would always leave after working about six hours. He probably spent another six hours or more at the executive office. I remembered having second thoughts about having his position. I didn't think I wanted an executive office anymore.

Before I went there, Sal (my former GM) jokingly stated that A.J. didn't work that many hours. He said that A.J. was always hanging out with his brother and his cousin. I thought it was shady that Sal was hating on A.J. because he was barely at work after 2:00 p.m. either. Sal wasn't going to an office; he was going to go play golf. I knew this because he would take other team members with him to go golfing. Definitely shady!

Other managers would also tell me that A.J. didn't work a lot and that he always went out of town. They would all say that you would never see A.J. at the restaurant after 2:00 p.m. After working with him, I realized they were all just jealous of him. He was such a great guy. By the way, no other general manager or manager had to split time working at the restaurant and the executive office.

One day, he came in to work and was about to leave around 2:00 p.m. When he went out to get his car, it had been stolen. He seemed defeated about this. The police came to the restaurant and did a police report. A.J. was beside himself. This was a decent area! He could not remember the last time someone had their car stolen in this area. He was upset, and I told him that I could drop him off at home. He told me not to worry about it. His daughter was on the way to pick him up. He said she would take him to the office and pick him up as well. Wow, what dedication! He had his car stolen but he was still going to make sure he made it to his office.

Later, the police contacted A.J. and advised him they had located his car. It was not stolen at all. A.J. had been working so much at the executive office, he had forgotten that he stopped at the grocery store next door before he came to work. A.J. would oftentimes walk next door to play his lottery and get a sweet tea. He did this several times a week, so on this day, when he went to the grocery store, he just walked out and went to the restaurant like he always did. He completely forgot that he drove to the store that morning before work.

When the police advised A.J. they found his car, he was elated. When they told him where they found it at, he was embarrassed. They told him the car had been running the entire day. A few of the other workers teased him about this mistake. I didn't tease him at all for this. As much time that he was spending at the executive office, it was no wonder he made a mistake. They were truly overworking this man.

Dejected, he looked at us and stated, "I'm going to get some gas and head to the office."

I wondered why he stopped at the gas station so often. He must've been spending a lot of money going to the executive office because he would oftentimes tell me that he had to go and get gas first. How far away was this place?

* * *

I was now six weeks into training, and the time had flown by. I only had two more weeks of training and that would be it. In the seventh week they sent you to Maryland, where our corporate office was located. The eighth week, you would finish your training and complete all your final certifications at the training restaurant. I was pumped up to go to Maryland. I had never been before, and this was the first time that someone would be paying for me to go anywhere. I felt like a big shot for the first time.

To my surprise, the day before I was going to fly out for Maryland, A.J. advised me that we would both leave early and stop by the executive office. I was pumped. I could hardly contain myself and had an extra pep in my step. I made sure to complete every task that I needed to complete on time. I didn't want anything to get in the way of us getting out of there early.

Unfortunately, time was going by extremely slow. You know how it is when you are anticipating something—the clock was moving as if time were standing still. It didn't help that I was looking at the clock every five minutes. I started getting antsy once 2:00 p.m. came. This was usually the time A.J. would leave.

I knew that any second, he would walk up to me and tell me that it was time for us to go. As I kept looking for him to come, time was still moving and no A.J. Business started to pick up and I still hadn't seen A.J. I knew I wouldn't be able to leave early while it was busy. I looked up and it was now 3:00 p.m. I started to get disappointed. I thought that maybe A.J. had forgotten about me and left. I finally asked one of the other managers if they had seen A.J. and they stated he was in the manager's office on a conference call. I felt relieved that he hadn't forgotten about me.

I continued to work and started to become dejected. It was now 5:00 p.m. and I was still at the restaurant. A.J. was still there as well. I had never seen A.J. in the building after 2:00 p.m. unless it was a general manager meeting, and now it was 5:00 p.m. Just as I was starting to lose hope on seeing the executive office, A.J. came up to me with his jacket on and told me that is was time to go.

I was happy again, although I felt sorry for him. He had been at the restaurant an entire shift already and still had to go to the executive office. I was hoping that he was just going to give me a tour and I would be in and out in a half hour. I had to fly out to Maryland early the next morning, so I didn't want to be at his office working for several more hours.

As we were walking out the door, I said my goodbyes and A.J. told me to follow behind him as the executive office was nearby. I was a little disappointed that it was nearby. I hadn't seen anything in the area that seemed like a corporate building, let alone a tall skyscraper-type building. I went ahead and followed A.J. as we drove about two miles away from the Blue Crab. He pulled into the parking lot of a restaurant called Beer Time. On top of the restaurant was a giant clock with mugs of beer representing the numbers on the clock. I was confused about why he stopped here first. I think someone said that his brother worked at this bar. Surely, A.J. was stopping here to drop something off for him.

I sat in the car and decided that I would wait for him while he ran in. A.J. was on his way into the restaurant when he paused. He looked back to see where I was at. Once he spotted me, he waved at me to come inside. Great, he must've wanted me to meet his brother. I really didn't want to go in. We were wasting time. I just wanted to get to the executive office before it was too late.

Reluctantly, I got out the car and went inside with A.J. Once inside, I saw that it was a cool place. It had television screens everywhere, with sports on every channel. The servers were all pretty girls with low-cut cheerleading outfits on. A.J. walked up to the bar and had a seat, so I followed. The bartender came from behind the bar and gave A.J. a long hug. He introduced me to her, and she gave me a cheerful hug as well. She was extremely friendly and perky, just like a cheerleader. She was just missing her pom-poms. She ran behind the bar and poured two tall beers and a shot of Jameson's and placed them in front of me and A.J. I looked at her name tag because I wanted to thank her. However, her name tag read "Brother." I was a little confused, so I just said *thank you*.

As A.J. and I started talking, I noticed that he downed his beer quickly. As soon as he put his mug down, the bartender, Brother, had another beer replacing it.

A.J. went over what I should expect when I got to Maryland. He told me to be smart when I got there and to avoid making friends. He also told me that people sometimes got fired when they were there. He said they tended to party too much and get drunk. Kind of reminded me of his restaurant, I thought. A.J. told me to make him proud while I was there and to be a leader.

Now, I was trying to pay attention to what A.J. was saying, but I was starting to realize that we were never going to make it to the executive office. As we were sitting there, more of the cheerleader workers started coming over to say hello. All their name tags had a weird name. Some were named Cousin, Gas, Out of Town, The Game, My Boys, The Gym, and Basketball. A.J. knew each one of these servers. I asked him why they had these weird names. A.J. told me that the restaurant's funny theme was based off giving excuses to the wife or girlfriend on where the patrons were going. This is what the names on the different tags represented. Brother meant you told your wife that you were hanging out with your brother. Gas was, "Honey, I'm going to get some gas." Honey, I'm going out of town, or to the game, to the gym, hanging out with my boys, or going to play basketball …

As A.J. was explaining this concept to me, I noticed that the restaurant was segmented into different themes. One section of the restaurant had a sign overhead that said Mancave. Another section was titled Bowling Alley. The next was Golf Range. It wasn't until I read the last sign that I started to put things together. The sign over the section where I was sitting with A.J. read "EXECUTIVE OFFICE."

It all started to make sense to me. It was like I was part of the movie *Usual Suspects*. A.J. had used everything in here as cues to what he did daily. I looked at him and he was already laughing at me. I said, "Dude, please don't tell me this is the executive office that you are always speaking about?"

A.J. looked at me, raised his beer mug, and said, "Yep, never miss a day." He chuckled, as he was obviously amused that I finally got it. He then stood up and called Brother. He gave her some cash and slapped me on the back. He said, "Have a good time in Maryland, kid. Be a leader. Make me proud!" And then he left me sitting at the bar to ponder my thoughts.

I had to laugh at myself. I was laughing and mad at the same time. A.J. had played me. I had felt sorry for this man for working so much. I even defended him when other people talked badly about him. I really thought that he was going to an executive office. The joke was truly on me.

I got up to leave. Brother came and gave me a hug and said she looked forward to seeing me again. I said goodbye and left. As I walked out the restaurant and got into my car, I told myself that I for sure didn't want to work for A.J. or this Blue Crab!

Leo

T he next day, I boarded my flight to Maryland for my completion of the management training. I was still fuming at A.J. for the executive office stunt, but I remembered him telling me to have a good time but not too much fun. I had heard stories about people getting drunk and sleeping together while there. I had learned my lesson from A.J.'s restaurant. No hanging out together. I was there to finish my training, and that was it.

The flight was uneventful. I had a cocktail to calm my flying nerves and went to sleep. After arriving in Maryland, I saw a few other people at the airport with Blue Crab CIT paraphernalia on. There were also Blue Crab signs in the airport that directed us to where our bus would pick us up.

As we made it to the bus and began to pile on, a Blue Crab representative greeted us. "Hello, everyone, and welcome to Maryland! I hope everyone is here to learn and have a great time. My name is Leonardo, but everyone just calls me Leo!" He shook our hands as we boarded the bus. He seemed quite young to be from our corporate office. I found a solo seat toward the back of the bus, put my headphones on, and attempted to get comfortable.

After the bus got rolling, Leo came around to talk to everyone. I wasn't in the mood to talk, but I also didn't want to seem anti-social. To my surprise, just before he got to me, one of the ladies on the bus, as she was laughing, shouted out, "Man, leave everybody alone and come sit yourself down." I was in shock that someone would talk to him in that manner.

I waited to see what would happen next. Leo walked toward her. "Excuse me young lady, are you speaking to me?" Leo looked serious before breaking out into laughter. "Crystal, you are always ruining my fun." Leo sat down next to Crystal and they laughed some more. Apparently, they were friends, and more apparent, Leo was not one of the corporate leaders but just a trainee just like the rest of us. A few of the others on the bus thought this was hilarious and they all shared in conversation with Leo and Crystal, but I steered away. I did not want to make any new friends, plus this Leo seemed like an idiot.

After checking in to the hotel, some of the CITs and Leo decided to hook up later and go to the bar. I knew better than to do this. I kept it moving and went to my room and checked in.

Training started the next morning at 7:00 a.m. The itinerary stated that we had to be in the hotel lobby at 6:30 a.m. We were told not to bring anything with us to the classroom. Everything would be provided. So, I walked to the lobby empty handed. Mostly everyone was in the lobby. There were more people than I thought there would be. There was twenty-four of us, to be exact. We were all excited; however, some people did not look too good. You could tell these were the ones who hung out drinking too late. Leo looked the worse of everyone. I was glad that I declined.

We were all assigned a van to get on. There were three Blue Crab vans in all waiting for us. I was on the bus with Leo, but he didn't say a word. Matter of fact, he fell asleep on the ride over. Fortunately for us, the ride to our corporate office was only about ten minutes.

As we filed into the building, our facilitators were waiting in the lobby to greet us. They took us for a quick tour of our corporate office. We saw the Blue Crab's test kitchen, the president's office, the call center, all meeting areas, and ended at the cafeteria. Once we were all situated in the cafeteria, we had assigned seats designated for us to sit at. As we found our seats, we were able to go up and get our breakfast.

After breakfast, we went to our meeting room, where once again we had assigned seats. At the seat, we were provided a book bag, pens, pencils, a stapler, a ruler, folders, and our crab master's in training booklet. Of course, all of this had the Blue Crab logo printed on it. As the facilitators came back into the room, they had us all stand. They told us we were going to learn the Blue Crab mission statement. They handed us laminated cards that we were told to bring with us every day we came into training. Our mission statement was also posted on every wall as well as on the front cover of our Blue Crab folder. We were instructed to put our hand over our heart as we read our mission statement out loud.

OUR MISSION STATEMENT

THE BLUE CRAB WANTS TO BE YOUR CHOICE FOR EVERYDAY DINING. WE GUARANTEE THAT YOU WILL RECEIVE TOP OF THE LINE FOOD AND SERVICE. OUR FOOD WILL BE FRESH, HOT, AND TASTY. OUR SERVICE WILL BE EXCELLENT AND BEYOND MEASURE. THIS AGAIN IS OUR GUARANTEE TO YOU.

After we quoted our mission statement, we were told that we would quote this every day at the beginning and the end of each class. They wanted us to embody what it meant to be a Blue Crab Master. I thought that it was a little cheesy that we had to put our hand over our heart. I could tell by looking at some of the others that they also thought it was a little cheesy. Leo made a spectacle out of it. He was the first one standing and the loudest by far. They made us repeat our mission statement at least three times a day until the training was over.

The training was long and exhausting, but some of the CITs still found time to hang out late drinking. Two of the trainees were fired before the end of the week. They had partied too much the night before. Some of the trainees were staying out until almost 3:00 a.m. I could not imagine staying out that late and drinking, knowing that I had to be up in a few hours. Their partying resulted in them oversleeping the next day and missing class.

The last day of training, we had a blast. We were to fly out first thing the next morning, so they wanted us to have fun. We only spent a few hours in the classroom while we got our certifications. They gave us graduation caps and a Blue Crab Diploma. The diploma stated that we were now certified Blue Crab Masters. We were elated and relieved that training was over. They encouraged us to go out and have fun on this last day. They gave us money to go to the bar at the hotel and relax. They told us to be smart and to not do anything stupid. We all made the promise that we would be on our best behavior. Before we departed, they made sure that we chanted the Blue Crab mission statement one more time. On this last day, everyone willingly had their hand to their chest and proudly quoted the mission statement. They did a good job engraining the mission statement in us!

As we left, the facilitators gave us high-fives and hugs. They told us they would see us off the next morning in the hotel lobby. We were all tired and decided to go rest and would meet at the bar around 7:00 p.m. We learned from the other two trainees that were fired not to take it too far. I decided to go back to my room and get some rest before I headed to the bar.

All our days lasted from six thirty in the morning until almost 9:00 p.m. I did not see how some of the others managed time to drink and party. I was exhausted after each day. Heck, I was still exhausted on the rest day and I was looking forward to getting some more rest. As I did each day of the training, as soon as I got to my room, I got out of my work clothes and sprawled across the bed. I watched television for about an hour and then I took a nap.

Once I got up from my nap, I showered and put on some casual clothes. This was the first time that we did not have to be dressed in slacks and a tie. I felt relieved. Once I got down to the bar, most of the team was already down there drinking. I was in disbelief how much these people enjoyed their alcohol. As soon as I walked up, Crystal gave me a shot of tequila! I downed it, but then she tried to offer me another one. I declined the offer. I was going to pace myself out and only have a couple. I did not know these people like this and was not about to get wild and loose with them. Leo and Crystal had come down a couple of hours before the rest of us. They were already wasted before 7:00 p.m. I guess they didn't learn from the other people that got fired earlier in the week. Those two were the loudest of the bunch.

Leo was uncontrollable, however. Everyone tried calming him down, but it was too late. At this point he was down to his T-shirt and swinging his jacket over his head. I just shook my head. What he did next was beyond stupid, though. We all knew that he was diabetic because he would talk about it every day. He said that he had to give himself an insulin shot every day to control the diabetes.

Well today, this idiot thought it would be funny to act like he was giving himself a shot in the veins. "Hey, guys, watch this! I am going to freak out this bartender chick. This bitch had the nerve to cut me off. Said I had too much to drink." We told him to calm down and to not do anything else stupid. He would not listen and went up to the bartender anyway.

"Hey. Since I can't have another drink, can I at least have a spoon so I can eat something?" Leo stated rudely. The bartender reluctantly gave it to him. Leo snatched the spoon from her and went back to the table. He then poured some vodka that he managed to steal from someone else onto the spoon and walked back up to the bar. Once at the bar, he used a lighter to light up the spoon. He took out one of his needles that he used for insulin and inserted it into the spoon.

The bartender looked at Leo and yelled, "Get out of my bar, now!" Leo, however, was too far into his stupidity act to stop now. The bartender thought that it was drugs on the spoon as Leo injected the vodka into the needle. He then used his shirt as a tourniquet to wrap his arm tight. This fool started acting as if he were about to inject himself with the needle. At this point, the bartender picked up the phone to call the hotel security. We all told Leo to get out of here immediately. We expressed to him that if the Blue Crab found out about this incident, he would be fired. Leo screamed out, "Fuck the Blue Crab!"

That was enough for me. I quickly paid my bill and left. Others did the same thing as well. As we were walking out, hotel security was walking in. I minded my business and kept walking.

As I was getting on the elevator, I saw one of the Blue Crab facilitators getting off another elevator. She had on her pajamas and a housecoat with slippers. She looked furious! I just looked the other way as I pushed the button to go up to my room. I wanted no part of that situation.

The next morning, we met each other in the lobby to get back to the airport. While we were waiting on our vans to arrive, everyone started talking about Leo. It was said that he was arrested that night. The hotel security had contacted the local police and Leo was crying like a baby as he was handcuffed. Leo was pleading with the facilitator to help him out, but there was nothing she could do. She ended up having to go down to the police station for his booking. Once it was determined that it was not drugs in the needle, they let Leo go. The word is, our facilitator advised Leo at the police station that he was terminated from the Blue Crab, effective immediately. They had canceled his flight and offered him a bus ticket to get back to his destination. I just shook my head and said, "What an idiot."

ҠASSAUNDRA!

Fortunately, when I came back from Maryland, I was given the next two days off. I needed the time to disengage from the Blue Crab. I was back at A.J.'s restaurant that Monday. I was still angry with him for the executive office stunt. When I saw him, he said no word of it. I asked A.J., "Are you going to talk to Chris today? I would love to know which location I am going to be working at." I was hoping that it wasn't going to be here with A.J. after that executive office joke.

"Yes, I talked to Chris, but I still don't know where you are going to be located, but he will be coming to the restaurant today. I'm sure he will let you know," exclaimed A.J. I thought he was lying to me again. I thought he knew exactly where I was going, but he didn't want to tell me. I was anxious to find out where I would be working at starting the next week.

Chris ended up coming in a few hours later. We sat down and spoke about my experience in Maryland. He already knew about the situation with the people that were terminated while in training. He told me that he was proud of me for not getting mixed up with the group.

He then laid out the rest of the week for me. He told me that I was going to spend two more days here with A.J. and then two days with Jackson at her restaurant. I slipped and said, "Great, the hyper lady!" I knew immediately that I had messed up.

Chris did not play when it came to his general managers. You never heard him say anything negative about them. He looked at me seriously and said, "If you don't want to work with her, you can go back to being a server."

I said, "Geesh, Chris, I was just kidding." He did not smile or show any sense that he thought what I said was funny.

He continued, "After the two days with Jackson, you will report to the Blue Crab in Hamtramck to work as a manager. Your general manager will be Kassaundra."

Oh no, not B.T.! I almost threw up in my mouth. *Not this Grizzly Bear Chick*, I thought. I was glad I made the mistake of saying the negative statement about Jackson. Had I not, I probably would have got fired for what I wanted to say about Kassaundra.

I just gritted my teeth and said, "Great, I look forward to working for her." Not only did I not want to work for her, but I did not want to work in Hamtramck. It could be rough in this area, just outside of Detroit.

Chris said, "Great, you can tell her yourself. She is meeting me up here to go over some things. She should be here in a few minutes."

I attempted to smile, although it was a stain more than a smile. I said, "Great, I can't wait to talk to her."

A few minutes later, B.T. indeed came walking into the building. She walked, I mean *stomped*, right passed me and barely spoke. It almost came out as a growl. I had to be careful what I asked for. I suddenly forgave A.J. and his executive office stunt. I would have rather worked with A.J. than this mean lady.

B.T. and Chris spoke for about a half hour. Afterward, B.T.

spoke with A.J. I knew they were talking about me. I did not know if she was aware that I was going to be working for her before today. She seemed upset about something. But then again, she always had that sour-puss look. As she was getting ready to leave, I walked up to her and attempted small talk.

Being careful not to say B.T., I said "Hi, Kassaundra, how are you today?" She never stopped to speak—she just continued to walk. I walked side by side with her, trying to keep up! I was almost in a light jog. I stated, "I look forward to working with you."

Before I could say anything else, she interrupted and said, "Great, I will see you next week! And by the way, you will not be working with me, you will be working *for* me!" and she kept walking right out the door. It was confirmed: I already regretted going to work for her. What an asshole!

FIRST DAY AS A MANAGER

I must admit, I was a little nervous. I had never been a manager before and now this was my first official day. The last eight weeks of training were not that difficult. A.J.'s restaurant on the surface looked great, but they had their fair share of skeletons. Well, the training was over and now I was reporting to my new restaurant for the first time.

I heard from other people that this restaurant could be tough to operate. I had already heard stories about rude and hostile guests as well as the same for some of the workers. I always try to stay neutral to other people's opinion. I like to form my own opinion about things instead of listening to someone else. It didn't help, however, that I was going to be working with B.T. *Okay, I better stop thinking of her as B.T. and call her Kassaundra. That is a lot more professional than B.T.* I had never called her B.T. to her face in the past, and I didn't want it to slip out one day.

I arrived at 9:45 a.m. for my first shift that started at 10:00 a.m. I got out the car, made sure I looked good, and walked toward the front door. As I approached, the door swung open as if someone was waiting for me to get here. It was Kassaundra! I sighed, put on a fake smile, and took a deep breath as I spoke. "Good morning, Kassaundra," I awkwardly said.

Surprisingly, she had a pulse and said, "Hello, Carter, and welcome to Hamtramck." This time it was no grunt or snarl as she said hello. I felt a small glimmer of hope that maybe she had a personality. I walked into the restaurant feeling slightly relieved.

"Carter, we are just finishing up having a kitchen meeting. I had everyone stay put so I can introduce you to everyone before we conclude." Walking into the room, I was nervous yet excited to meet my new team. "Everyone, this is Carter! This is the new manager I was telling you about. Introduce yourself and let's get back to work!" Kassaundra stated.

As I was going around shaking hands and asking the employees to repeat their names for me, one of the kitchen employees introduced themselves to me and asked me if they could borrow five dollars. I was caught off guard by this. I told him that I could not loan out any money. He laughed at me and said he was just kidding. I laughed with him, but in the back of my mind I was hoping this is not how things would go at this location. I was not going to be loaning any money to anyone.

After I met everyone, Kassaundra briefly showed me around and then brought me to the office. "Carter, I have a few things to work on, but I want you to get started right away. Have you done a pre-opening checklist before?" she asked.

I had done the checklist so many times during training that I confidently stated, "Yes, I have!"

She shoved a clipboard at me and said, "Great, get started on it now."

A pre-opening checklist is a thorough check of the restaurant before it opens. This includes taking temperatures of coolers, checking restrooms, rotating product, etc. I completed this daily when I was in training, so I knew just what to do. I started out in the dining room first and then came into the kitchen afterward.

Everything was going normal until I came to the cook line and started taking temperatures. I noticed that the cook had a whole bag of frozen french fries still in the bag, just sitting in the fry basket over the fryers. I asked her what she was doing with the fries and she said, "Don't worry, I got it, honey!" I advised her that our french fries are cooked frozen and couldn't just sit here thawing out over the fryers! She said, "Don't get your little panties in a bunch, I got it." I was floored. Wow, first the guy asking me for five dollars, now this.

"Hey, listen, you need to take care of this now and don't ever speak to me like that again," I barked back. The cook turned around ready for a fight, but Kassaundra approached.

"Carter, don't worry about it. She has it under control. Just finish doing your checklist."

I started thinking that maybe I made a bad decision going into management. I had already seen managers get disrespected at A.J.'s restaurant, and now I was seeing it on the first day here. It was disheartening to see that the employees acted in this manner at this location as well. Furthermore, instead of my boss having my back, she allowed for this lady to completely undermine me.

The cook was a little person. She must've been about four feet tall but she was not friendly. She was mean and unprofessional, just like Kassaundra. This was totally unacceptable to me. I had no idea this would be a sign of things to come and that it would become worse than that.

Well, it got worse quickly! We were only open for about an hour and things were going relatively smoothly. Suddenly, one of the servers came running up to me, panicking.

"My table just walked out on their bill without paying," she shouted.

Calmly, I asked, "Are you sure the money wasn't left on the table or they didn't give it to another server?"

She looked as if I had just insulted her intelligence. "Carter, that's your name, right?"

I nodded.

"Do you think I would've come and got you if they paid? I assure you there is no money on that table."

I asked her, "How long ago was it since these guests left?"

She told me they just left. "Follow me," I said as I went to the front of the restaurant to see if we could catch them before they got out the building. They were already gone, but as we looked out of the windows, the server noticed the customers were getting in their car.

"That's them, right there getting into the silver Jeep," she belted, garnering attention from the entire restaurant.

I told her, "Hand me their check and I will take it from here."

I walked outside and approached the silver Jeep. The customers looked startled and confused when they saw me standing there. It was one guy and two ladies in the Jeep. The driver, who was the guy, rolled his window down and asked me, "What's going on?"

I thought to myself, *Really, asshole, you know what's going on, you didn't pay for your bill*. I stayed professional, however, as I said, "Sir, I was advised by the server that we did not receive payment for your bill. Here is your receipt. I will gladly go and process your payment for you."

He looked even more confused. "Sir, I don't know what your server told you, but she was taking too long and we have to get back to work, so we left the cash inside the check holder thing she gave us."

He must've thought I was a damn fool. "Sir, I'm sorry, but we did not receive your payment."

As I was talking, he shook his head at me and frowned, rolled his window back up, and pulled out of his parking space. As they were pulling past me, I walked behind their vehicle and wrote down their license plate. One of the ladies in the backseat rolled her window down and screamed, "What are you doing?"

I told her, "You know what I am doing! I am writing down your license plate number and will hand it to the police. I will let them handle it." She gave me the finger and then they screeched out of the parking lot. I was angry they didn't just pay for the bill. Why run out on a bill? If you ordered it, just pay for it.

I couldn't wait to get in the restaurant and call the police. I was going to show everyone around here that when I was on duty, I was not to be played with. This went for the employees and the customers. As I walked back in the restaurant, feeling like a superhero for confronting those thieves, the server came running back up to me. I told her, "No problem, I didn't get the money, but I did get their license plate. They will be paying for this one way or another."

The server looked at me sheepishly and stated, "My bad. When you went outside, I went back over to the table and found the money. It was placed in between two of their plates and I didn't see it."

"My bad?" I yelled. "You told me there wasn't any money on the table. I just accused these people of stealing."

She looked at me and shrugged as she said, "Damn, I said my bad!"

I just looked at her and wanted to strangle her. I was ashamed that I confronted those guests when they did nothing wrong. They would probably never come back to eat here again. Furthermore, I hope they didn't call our corporate office on me. I decided quickly that I was going to go work in the kitchen for the remainder of lunch. I didn't feel comfortable working in the dining room with this crew on my first day.

Luckily for me, no tables needed a manager and I was able to stay in the kitchen. The mean cook was moving fast and barking orders to everyone else. She would stand on a step stool to assemble the food and so she could bark through the cookline at the servers. After we got through a steady lunch shift, with me working in the kitchen with the mean cook who seemed as if she was running the restaurant, things started to slow down a little.

Around 3:00 p.m., the two-night shift managers came in to work their shift. There was one other manager that worked here as well, but he was off today. I worked in the morning with Kassaundra. She wanted to make sure that I was properly acclimated to the restaurant. What a joke! Anyway, when the two other managers came in, Kassaundra had me sit down with them to have a late lunch and to get acquainted.

As I sat down with the other managers, they both introduced themselves to me. The first person to talk to me was named Franklin. Now, I had met Franklin before when I was a server. I had filled in at a Blue Crab that he used to be at for a weekend because they were short staffed due to a wedding someone in the restaurant was having. He came into the kitchen dancing, wearing a pink cowgirl hat and pink heels. They were having a contest with the bartenders and he was trying to get everyone excited.

I told him how I had met him once before, but he couldn't

recall. I told him that he had on the pink heels and was dancing. Franklin said, "I still can't remember. Shit, that could've been yesterday!" Without notice, Franklin started singing a Patti LaBelle song and swaying to the beat in his head. I stared in disbelief.

The other manager that introduced themselves to me was named Momma—really, *Momma* was what everyone called her. She should've been ashamed of herself for using that nickname at a place of business as a manager. It even said *Momma* on her business cards. Momma was kind of quiet and didn't say much, although when she did talk, half her words were curse words! Momma had to be about seventy years old. She was tall and grumpy, with a crooked wig on, and she smelled like coffee and Newport cigarettes.

As we were sitting there, eating our meal, one of the servers came over and introduced herself to me. I told her my name was Carter and that I was the new manager. She said, "Hey Carter, nice to meet you. My name is Alexandria, but everyone calls me Bitch!" I was shocked that she had the audacity to speak like this in the restaurant. I was not only sitting with two other managers, but we were also in the dining room. Any one of our customers could have heard her.

I was quick to chastise her and set the standard. I looked at her and said in my stern voice, "Young lady, we will not tolerate any language like this in the restaurant. This is a family restaurant and we will be professional at all times." She looked at me, astonished. I knew that I had made my point. She was speechless. I thought to myself that she was about to find out who was in charge very quickly.

Franklin and Momma didn't say a word. They kept eating and grinning at each other. I was a little upset they did not chime in, but it did not matter. The server was still standing there with her mouth open. Just when I thought that her mouth was stuck, she burst out in laughter. She looked at Franklin and Momma and said, "Aww, y'all got a newbie, straight out the box. He so cute. I'm going to have to potty train him." Alexandria and the two managers broke out into laughter.

I sat there thinking, *Wow, what a bitch!*

Besides the Bitch and the mean cook, most of the morning crew was nice and approachable. As I introduced myself to others, most of them were respectable and said hello.

There was one more server that I immediately knew I didn't care for. Her name was Malorie and she was borderline rude. After I introduced myself, she just rolled her eyes and walked off. I wanted to smack her upside the head. I found out that she had been working here for almost six years. If this was her attitude daily, how could Kassaundra let her work as a server?

Besides Malorie, I was floored to find out the mean cook had also been working at this Blue Crab for ten years already. There were also some other ladies who had been here for over ten years as well. They really knew how to do their job and didn't require a lot of attention. To think about it, there weren't too many guys working at the time except for in the kitchen. The guy that asked me for five dollars was in the kitchen. I stayed away!

In the front was one more guy. He was a host named Jack. Jack was a short and chubby Black man. He looked to be around forty years old. He always kept himself poised and always wore a suit jacket. All the servers listened to Jack. Jack ran the front of the restaurant just as good as any manager I had ever seen.

As I finished up my lunch with Momma and Franklin, I went back into the kitchen. Most of the morning crew was leaving for the day and the night crew was starting to filter in. I found out quickly that the night crew was completely different than the day crew. Unfortunately, Kassaundra had to leave a little early. Now if she told me that she was going to an executive office, I would have blown my top. I would never fall for something like that again. If A.J. was going to a bar, then B.T. (oops, Kassaundra) had to be going to a crack house.

Once Franklin and Momma came in and got settled, she left. You could tell the difference almost immediately. After we sat down and ate, Momma and Franklin went outside to smoke. It seemed as if they stayed outside for about a half hour smoking and talking. This left me inside to manage the changeover of the shifts. Luckily, Jack told me that he would take care of the dining room for me. I told Jack that I could do it, but he insisted. He told me that he always ran the front of the house and that I never needed to worry about that. This just left me to check out the kitchen crew before they left.

Checking out the kitchen was harder than I thought. Now, the mean morning cook (I found out that her name was Jasmine) could cook fast, but she left her area a hot mess. As soon as the night cook came in, Jasmine grabbed her things to leave without attempting to clean up.

I tried to stop her from leaving. "Jasmine, I need you to clean your area before you leave," I stated.

She said, "Honey, I got to go! I don't stay a minute past four!"

"What about your workstation? It's a disaster," I replied.

"Listen, honey, I have to go. If you have a problem with this, then talk to Kassaundra." She even had one of our stepstools folded and carried it out the door with her. I was furious, but I was not about to fight with this lady. I decided that I would inform Franklin and Momma about her when they came in.

When they came back into the building, I immediately told them what happened. They both looked at me like it was no big deal. Franklin told me that it was okay and that she always left at this time. I told him that she even walked out with one of our step stools. Franklin just laughed and told me that it was hers. She wasn't tall enough to reach some of the microwaves above the cook line, so she brought it with her every day.

Momma just looked at me and walked away. She was very anti-social. It was hard to believe that she was a manager. I hadn't really heard her say more than a few words. Franklin told me not to worry about it. He was the kitchen manager and he told me that he could whip the kitchen into shape immediately.

For all his unprofessional ways, he did know what he was doing in the kitchen. He was able to get the kitchen organized in about thirty minutes. It was impressive. However, he talked to his people like he was out on the street. He told this one girl to clean out the microwaves that were on the upper shelf. The girl was a little on the heavy side and was going to have a hard time reaching up there. The young lady told Franklin that she couldn't reach up that high. What Franklin said next floored me.

He looked at the girl and said, "You better climb your fat ass up on that table and clean that microwave." I was speechless as I looked at Franklin and the young lady. The young lady said nothing, but she climbed up on the table and started cleaning the microwave. Everyone was laughing at this, but I walked away.

As Franklin stayed in the kitchen, I worked out front with Momma. I have no idea in this world what purpose she served as a manager. She hated people and avoided the guests like a plague.

When the night shift servers came in, Momma wouldn't check them in or let them know what we were featuring for the day. She would just tell them they better not have any damn complaints. From my observation, she was horrible. She was just here to lock the door and count the money. She was in the wrong line of work. She should've been working somewhere where she didn't have to engage with people. She would also curse a lot as well. She wasn't as bad as Franklin when it came to cursing, but no one was. She didn't necessarily curse at people, but more at the situation. If a server asked her to go to a table because they had a complaint, her response would be, "Aw, fuck!"

I had never seen anything like these two managers. It became worse once the day crew left and the night crew came on. The night crew came in with the mindset of partying. Why wouldn't they? Franklin had the same mindset and Momma didn't care what they did. Most of the crew that came in seemed to have an attitude. Unlike the morning cook, the night cooks couldn't care less if their food came out fast or not. They all moved slow and had no pep in their step. Franklin came back to the cook line a few times and told them they must "Fuckin move faster." The main cook for the night shift, Angie, told Franklin to "Settle your ass down, the food is coming." Again, I couldn't believe this behavior.

Unlike Momma, Franklin introduced me to everyone as they were coming in to work. He kept telling everyone that I was the newbie manager and that he was going to show me the ropes around here. Looking at the roster report, I had met everyone that was working for the night except for this one server named Maria. She was supposed to be at work at five thirty. It was now six o'clock and she still wasn't at work.

Around six thirty she came strolling in with her mug of

coffee. Who drinks a huge mug of coffee at six thirty in the evening? Maria was a short, attractive, and curvaceous Mexican girl. Although she was attractive, she had a horrible attitude, which made her unattractive. As soon as Franklin saw her, he confronted her about being late.

Maria just threw her hand up at his face and said, "Uh-uh girl, not today." I thought it was funny that she called Franklin *girl*.

It didn't seem to bother Franklin one bit. Franklin said, "Your ass is always late. You need to be on time."

Maria said, "Cool, does that mean I can go home?"

As she started walking back toward the entrance door, Franklin barked, "Get your ass out to your section and get to work."

Maria then said, "Okay, but I will be sure to let Kassaundra know that you are using profanity toward me."

Franklin snarled, "Whatever!"

Maria then rambled something off in Spanish to him.

Franklin said, "And don't be speaking that Mexican language to me. You know I don't know that Spanish shit."

At first, I thought that Maria and Franklin were mad at each other, but then I sensed they had a playful banter between them. I was witnessing this and looking like a deer in the headlights. I had never seen anything like this. One of the more tenured servers came over to me and said they did this every day.

I observed Maria and Franklin playing back and forth with each other for the rest of the night. Maria was a good server and throughout the evening, several guests had asked to sit in her section. She almost doubled the number of tables that anyone else would have. I noticed that some of her fellow team members were upset about it. Maria was running six to seven tables, but everyone else had two. They would complain to each other about it, but not to Maria.

Maria was a good server, but she was abrasive. She could argue with the best of them. And win the argument. Momma never would confront her, and Franklin would fuss at her, but that was it. It was like Maria was running the night crew. The cooks would also give her whatever she wanted without giving her any pushback. I was surprised because the cooks had something nasty to say to everyone else. I had no idea how Maria was doing it, but no one gave her any problems. I still knew that I would eventually have a problem with her. I was not about to kiss her butt and answer to her.

Finally, around eight o'clock, both Franklin and Momma told me that I could leave. I was elated to leave. This place had me overwhelmed. In my entire time at the Blue Crab, I had never seen an operation like this one. I was second guessing what I got myself into. I went and got my things out of the office and walked around and said goodbye to everyone. I learned this from A.J. He was very personable with his team.

As I was saying goodbye, Maria came over, coffee mug in hand, and gave me a hug. Although I don't consider myself that tall, she was a lot shorter than me, so I had to bend over a little to hug her. I was surprised that she hugged me, but what was more surprising is that she smelled like liquor. The alcohol smell was extraordinarily strong. I didn't say anything at the time. It was my first day, but I knew she had to be drinking at work. I peeped that out early with the coffee mug. Who brings in a coffee mug to work at 6:00 p.m.? I didn't care, I just wanted to go home. I said goodbye and I left for the night.

Once I got home, I was restless. I processed the events of the day and as I thought about it, I began to wonder. Was I overwhelmed? Was this place too much? It was a lot to process. I decided to let it go. It was only day one. Surely, things would get better. I took a long hot shower and relaxed my mind. I wasn't going to give up this easy. Tomorrow, I was going into work and I would make it a great day. Proud of myself for my little pep talk, I jumped out of the shower, toweled myself off, slid on some shorts and a T-shirt, and went to sleep.

ͨTODAY WAS A GOOD DAY

The next day, I was scheduled to be at work from 3:00 p.m. to close. This was my first close and I was a little timid on closing by myself. Once I arrived, I felt a little relief. Kassaundra advised me, "Carter, I'm going to close with you. We have the same schedule for the rest of the week. They are all closing shifts. I want to make sure you know how to properly close the way I like it." I felt great relief with her closing with me. I had keys to the restaurant, the alarm code, the safe codes, as well as multiple passwords, but I didn't want to mess any of these things up.

While Kassaundra and I were in the office talking, the other manager that I hadn't met yet came walking into the office. He introduced himself and we shook hands. His name was Travis. Travis seemed to be in command and a serious individual. He carried himself like a police officer. He was tall and had a firm handshake. He politely interrupted our conversation to ask Kassaundra a question. After Kassaundra answered the question, Travis walked out of the office.

Kassaundra stated, "Carter, Travis is an excellent manager and you will spend a lot of time working with him. Travis is the service manager. You will also work in the same role with him as the co-service manager. Momma manages the bartenders and hosts, and Franklin is our kitchen manager." She also advised me that Travis had opened the restaurant this morning and that he would be doing some product orders and leaving in a couple of hours. She told me to go out front and manage the dining room and she would run the kitchen the entire night.

As I went to work the dining room, I went around and said hello to everyone. I didn't have too much to manage because Jack was hosting, and he had the restaurant running smoothly. The Bitch wasn't at work either, so it was all good. Travis took me around and introduced me to more people that I hadn't met on my prior shift. I found out quickly that this day was going to be a lot different than my first day. The restaurant ran completely different with Kassaundra and Travis in the building. Travis carried himself in a way that demanded respect and Kassaundra was the general manager, so everyone always followed her lead. I was grateful for having them in today. I truly couldn't handle another day like my first day.

Even the changeover of shifts was a lot better. Since Kassaundra was working the kitchen, she made sure mean Jasmine had everything cleaned up and set up for the night shift. She even seemed to be happy today, which I didn't think was possible. Jasmine even surprised me and said goodbye before she left. She also gave me a compliment on my pants, I think!

She said, "I love those pants!" She looked dreamy as she said it.

Oh no, I hope this mean chick doesn't like me. It felt awkward, but I said, "Thanks!"

As she walked past me, she grabbed my behind. I looked

down at her in shock that she was bold enough to do this. Before I could say anything, she winked at me and said, "Ooh and the pants feel even better than they look!"

I turned around to confront her, but I saw Kassaundra standing there. She had seen the entire thing. Surely, she was going to handle this. Instead, she burst into laughter and said, "Looks like Jasmine got her a new man!" I just walked away, shaking my head. *Note to self, do not ever wear these pants again!*

As I continued walking around, I went into the backroom at the restaurant. We called this area the anchor. We usually didn't seat the anchor until the weekend when it was busy. Other than that, the anchor would double as a breakroom slash interview room during the week. The room was segmented into two halves. In one half, the crew sat down and ate as well as stored their personal belongings. The second half would be where we conducted our manager meetings or gave interviews.

There were quite a few people hanging out in the anchor when I went back there. I introduced myself to a couple of people that were in the room. Someone said, "Fresh meat!" *What is this place—prison?* I thought. I just ignored them.

As I walked around to the other side of the room, I noticed a couple sitting in a booth. I was going to say hello, but I noticed that not only were they sitting side by side, but their eyes were closed. They were either praying or meditating, but I kept it moving and didn't say hello to either of them. I didn't want to interrupt.

I made it back to the main dining room and ended up working with Jack for about thirty minutes. I was amazed at how good he ran the floor. I had never seen another host or a manager who could run the dining room as efficiently as Jack. He knew a lot of customers by first name and they knew him as well. He didn't want to be a manager, but he had his own business cards that stated he was the dining room coordinator. He was truly this indeed. I also realized that although Jack was professional with the guests, he was a little on the messy side. He liked to talk about people. The good thing was that he would let you know how he felt. He didn't sugarcoat it or talk behind your back. The team respected Jack and would do whatever he told them.

Jack said he was about to get off work for the day. I asked him who was going to replace him. He told me that his replacement was already here. He told me that her name was Simone and that she was in the anchor. I told him that I was just in the anchor, but I didn't recall meeting anyone named Simone.

Jack said, "Man, she back there praying to Buddha, Allah, or Jesus Christ with one of her boyfriends."

I said, "One of her boyfriends?"

Jack said, "Yes, one of her boyfriends. Simone is an extremely sweet girl, but she confused. She got three different guys chasing after her and she don't know which one to pick."

At this moment, Simone came walking up. Jack said, "I was just talking about you and your three amigos!"

Simone looked at Jack and said playfully, "Shut up, Jack, don't start with me. Those are just my friends."

Jack said, "Don't tell me that, you need to tell them. Each one of them think they are your man, especially that boy that you were just praying with. Me and Darlene been married for twenty years and we don't pray like that together. Y'all looked intimate! Almost turned me on!"

Simone said, "We were not praying, we were meditating."

Jack said, "Yeah right, you might have been meditating, but he was praying. Praying about getting in your panties!"

Simone laughingly said, "Ugh Jack, you are so nasty!"

Jack said, "Whatever, Simone. Anyhow, meet Carter. This is our new manager. He started yesterday and will be working up front with you. Make sure to introduce him to everyone tonight and don't let them run you over, Simone." Jack looked at me and said goodbye to us both. As he was leaving, he stated that he was going home to meditate.

Simone replied, "Oh, that's cool. If you ever need any meditation music, let me know."

Jack said, "No thanks. I'm going to put on some Luther Vandross and meditate like your boyfriend. I'm going to meditate about getting in Darlene's panties."

Simone once again said, "Uuuuuggghh Jack, you are so nasty!" Simone gave him a hug and told him to say hello to Darlene.

I ended up working with Simone for the next couple of hours. She was a great person and overly sweet. She was easy to talk to and everyone that came in the door loved her. She had developed an individual rapport with each person that worked there. Simone had a carefree attitude. She let nothing bother her and she never bothered anyone. She was a breath of fresh air. Simone explained to me the difference between the day shift and the night shift and how the floor plan and the floor charts worked. She would even quiz me on table numbers.

I saw firsthand why Simone had so many dudes liking her. She was slightly flirtatious and extremely kind. I don't think there was a dude in there that wasn't low-key crushing on her a little bit. And that would include myself. I wasn't interested in dating her or anyone else that I worked with, but there was just something about her. I couldn't put my finger on what is was about her. She didn't wear any makeup or tight-fitting clothes. Besides being flirtatious, she was genuinely a nice person. Even Travis was putty in her hands. When Travis would come by to let us know something, she would smile at him and salute him! Although he was a serious man and military-like, he would smile back at her.

As Travis was about to leave, he made sure that I was set up for the rest of the dinner shift. It was ten minutes to six o'clock. Every server was there except for Maria. He asked me if I had seen Maria yet and I said no. She was already twenty minutes late. I could tell that Travis was irritated with this. He stated that he was going into the office to call her.

About five minutes later, Maria and her coffee mug came prancing into the restaurant. Travis was standing in the front, waiting on her. As soon as she walked in, she looked at Travis and rolled her eyes. She threw her hand up in the air and said, "Don't even start with me today!" She continued to walk past Travis as he was talking to her. He did not like this at all. He followed her into the kitchen, barking at her for being late. Much to my surprise, Maria didn't say anything.

A few minutes later, Travis came walking back out of the kitchen. He looked satisfied that he had put her in her place. He shook my hand and said goodbye and then he said goodbye to Simone. Of course, she gave him a hug! After he left, Simone explained to me that Travis was the only one who could slightly keep Maria in check. She said that Kassaundra couldn't even control Maria.

As the night went on, it was pretty uneventful. Maria was talking loudly and making fun of everyone that worked. I didn't see Kassaundra that much. She was hanging out in the office for most of the night. The few times that she would come out, Maria poked fun at her.

She would say, "Kassaundra, girl, where have you been? You must've been sleeping in the office! You going to leave the new manager to do all the work! You are so wrong!"

Kassaundra would look at her and tell her that she better watch herself. Maria would do nothing but laugh at Kassaundra. She then would say, "Well, I could go home if you want me to." Kassaundra would just walk away from her, completely unbothered by Maria's shenanigans.

Maria walked up to me, laughed, and said, "Don't nobody say nothing to me, they know that I run this!" As she was speaking to me, I confirmed it: this chick was drunk. You couldn't help but smell the alcohol on her breath. I knew that Kassaundra and Travis had to smell it as well. What was it about this chick that no one was going to say anything to her? Kassaundra must've still been okay with people being drunk at work, like she was in the earlier years when we used to work together.

Simone explained to me that Maria was the best server they had by far. She explained that although Maria was tough on people, she knew her stuff. Simone told me that on any given night, Maria would have a lot of call parties. Call parties are the same as a request party. This is when a guest only wants you to serve them. I used to have call parties when I was a server, but nothing like Maria.

As the night continued, we got a little busy and went on a small wait. There were people that would wait in the lobby for Maria if her section was full no matter how long the wait was.

As I observed Maria, I noticed that she was thorough, professional, and personable with her tables. She knew most of the guests by first and last name. She also did something that I could never do. She took every order by memory. She would never write an order down. I saw her take a table of seven by herself and she never wrote down a thing. It was quite impressive. To this day, if I take an order, I have to write down everything. If a guest asks for lemon with their water, I have to write that down. I was blown away that Maria could remember everything.

Toward the end of the night, Kassaundra came out of the kitchen and sat at the bar. She told me that she was going to sit there and let me close everything. At first, I was a little upset that she was going to just sit there and let me do all the work. She saw that I was a little irritated and she explained to me that she would be there to answer any questions I may have while closing. I was glad that she was, because I must've come up to her about twenty times. She told me this is the reason that she wanted me to do everything. It was better for me to learn and make mistakes while she was in the building, versus me making the mistakes when I was by myself. I completely understood her, although I had never seen another general manager do what she was doing. She had changed into some gym shoes and put a jacket and baseball cap on. She sat at the end of the bar drinking margaritas. I thought this was against the rules for the Blue Crab. I shook my head and said to myself, *Whatever.* It didn't concern me one bit.

The rest of the week, Kassaundra would continue to close with me. As per her norm, she would sit down at the end of the bar and drink her margaritas while I closed. I no longer gave it any thought that she stayed and drank every night. I was just grateful that she stayed with me. By the end of the week, I was satisfied that I could close by myself on any given night. On my last night closing with her, she gave me a beer, and she also gave one to the last cook and the dishwashers. I thought that it was cool. Today was a good day. Maybe Kassaundra wasn't that bad after all, I thought!

~Simone's Love Triangle

Besides working with Kassaundra every night my first week, I also worked with Simone every night. She was simply awesome. She really made it enjoyable to work here. I also saw in person what Jack was referring to. She really had three guys fighting over her.

The guy that I saw her praying or meditating with was completely into her. He was a little possessive and weird, though. His name was Jeremiah. Jeremiah was repetitious. He would come into work, clock in, and then go meditate. He would then go and flirt with Simone at the host podium as well as talk with the rest of the crew for about an hour. The problem was, he was the evening prep cook guy. He would spend the first two hours doing everything *but* prepping. About the time he would begin prepping, we would be busy and into our dinner shift.

Every night that he worked, we would be out of product. It didn't seem to bother Jeremiah at all. He was carefree and said that he was not going to let anything bother him. Although we were behind due to him, he never sped up his pace. He would also start cleaning up one hour prior to closing so that he wouldn't be there all night. Part of this was because he was trying to hurry up so that Simone could drop him off at home. He didn't drive and she was his ride home.

Meanwhile, Simone's other gentleman caller was one of our I.T. guys named Carlton. He was about twenty years older than Simone. Simone told me they used to date and that he was incredible, but he was also very possessive. She told me that he proposed to her, but she thought that she was too young to get married to him. Carlton's kids were almost the same age as Simone. He also didn't want her to work. He told her that she could just stay home, and he would take care of all her needs. Simone said it would be nice to not have bills, but she knew that she would be sitting home barefoot and pregnant if she got married to him.

Although we only had computer issues maybe once a week, Carlton surprisingly found a way to work on something in our restaurant every shift that Simone was there. We always had the most updated computer system. We all knew he was there to see Simone. She liked him a lot. She said it was tempting to take him up on his offer, but there was one problem.

Enter the third gentleman caller. This third guy was Jessie. He was Simone's first love. They had dated since middle school and had even went to prom together. Jessie treated Simone awful, but he was her first love and she wanted nothing more than to have a family with him. Jesse was also possessive! Now, even though he wanted nothing to do with Simone, he didn't want anyone else to have her either. From time to time, Jessie would come up to the restaurant to show his presence. He was like a predator marking his territory. A territory that he didn't even want.

Now, all three of the guys knew about each other. Although I think Simone liked Carlton and Jeremiah, I think unknowingly they were used as pawns to make Jessie jealous. Simone wanted nothing more than to marry Jessie and have a family with him. Simone seemed like a wonderful young lady, but having three grown men fighting for her love was ridiculous.

I had to be careful. In this short time, I was already attracted to Simone and I felt as if she was attracted to me. When she talked to me, she would gaze into my eyes. Maybe I was being a fool, but I thought she was into me.

TRAVIS

Although I didn't work that much with Travis during my first week, there was no doubt that he was second in charge behind Kassaundra. It was said that Travis would soon be a general manager. He was just waiting on a position to open for him. My following week, I did work quite a few shifts with him. Travis was well balanced in the restaurant. He was over the service area, but he knew the other areas just as well. He was able to go help at the bar in a pinch as well as go in the kitchen and help the line cooks. It was impressive!

What was more impressive was the way he controlled Maria. No one, not even Kassaundra, had control over Maria. Maria and her coffee mug continued to be late on every shift, but she didn't talk as much when Travis was around. Maria also made fun of every person that worked there, including every manager except Travis. Travis would yell at her for something and Maria would just drunkenly smile and say, "No problem, Big Daddy!"

Maria made it no secret that she liked Travis. She said that he was tall and handsome and always in control. She said that she loved tall men, despite not being tall herself. Maria always wore her shirt a little extra tight and with the top buttons unbuttoned. She also wore her pants very tight-fitting. Although she was loud and drunk, most men didn't mind. They were usually looking at her perky boobs and she knew it too. She was always flaunting them when she could. Travis would always tell her to button her shirt up. He didn't let Maria get away with anything. I overheard Maria saying to someone that she enjoyed having Travis tell her to button up. This way, she knew that he was looking.

There was another girl named Kenya who made it known that she liked Travis, but she wasn't as obvious when Maria was around. Maria didn't play around when it came to him. Kenya wasn't scared of Maria, but she didn't want to hear Maria's mouth. Kenya just flirted with Travis on Maria's off days.

While working with Travis, I noticed he would play no games with the crew or the guests. He was militant and professional and expected everyone to act accordingly. We were in a tough location and the guests could oftentimes be difficult and rude. Travis would take none of this behavior. I observed Travis put the guests in their place on several occasions.

The first time I saw this, I knew it was coming. For whatever reason, there was no hostess up front. When Travis walked past the lobby, he noticed there was a couple standing up front looking agitated. He quickly greeted them, "Hello, welcome to the Blue Crab. I apologize for your wait."

The young lady was not receptive to his apology. She ignored his comment as if he wasn't speaking. She rolled her eyes and stated, "Why weren't we greeted immediately? This makes no sense. There's hardly anyone in here!"

Travis was apologetic once again and explained, "Ma'am, our host must be seating someone else, but I can surely take you to your table right away." The gentleman that was with her shook his head and said that he was about to go to the bathroom. You could tell that he was embarrassed by her behavior and, apparently, she acted like this all the time. As the gentleman walked away, Travis grabbed the menus and once again apologized to the young lady and asked her to follow him. She just wouldn't stop complaining.

As he was walking her toward the table, she complained, "Why are you walking so fast?" Travis slowed his pace and again apologized.

He then got her to a table and she said, "No, I don't like this table."

Travis walked her to another table and she quickly denied that one as well. "Okay, ma'am, show me where you would like to sit." Although we were slow and had at least twenty other clean tables that were available, she picked a table that had just gotten up and still had dirty dishes on it. Travis grabbed a server and had them remove the dishes and then he grabbed a towel and wiped the table down himself.

When Travis finished wiping the table, the lady said, "Um, you missed a spot."

I could tell that he was starting to unravel. He sighed and wiped the mysterious spot that she said he had forgotten. Next, he sat the menus down, and she began on him again. She told him that he needed to open the menu and explain the special offers that we have. Travis had had enough. He looked at her and picked the menus back off the table and began to walk away. While he was walking away, the gentleman that was with her was walking toward the table.

She stood up and said, "Hey, where are you going with the menus?"

Travis said, "Oh, my bad, we will not be able to serve you. You have to leave."

She was agitated and said, "What?"

Travis said, "There is no way that I am going to allow you to sit down and eat here. If you are this rude with me, I can't imagine how rude you will be to one of our servers! Goodbye."

She tried to apologize, but Travis was done. He looked at her and her guy friend seriously and said "Goodbye!" They got the hint and left.

On another occasion, it was a Friday night and very busy. Travis ended up coming up to the host podium to help. As he was taking names, one of the male guests came up to him and started complaining about the wait. The guy started getting too loud and kept calling Travis *dawg*.

The guest kept saying, "C'mon, dawg, this wait is ridiculous."

"Hey dawg, how much longer will it be?"

"Dawg, can we sit at the bar?"

The last time the guest called him *dawg*, Travis just walked away from him midsentence.

The guest yelled out, "Hey, dawg, where you going?"

Travis spun around, looked squarely into the guest's eyes, and stated, "Sir, since we don't serve animals here, until you can address me properly, you will not be dining in here."

The guest stood there in bewilderment. Travis looked at the host and said, "Do not seat this gentleman as he has decided not to eat here." Travis just walked away.

✱ ✱ ✱

I'd seen Travis come and remove dinners from in front of guests. Oftentimes, servers would come and get me to talk to their tables because Travis was sometimes too abrasive. He would get quite a few complaints to our corporate office about him, but I don't think corporate or upper management was bothered by his abrasiveness at this location. It was tough to staff this location with managers because the location was rough. They knew that Travis was abrasive, but also that he was a good manager. Corporate didn't want to push Travis too much and have him leave.

There would be times that I would be in the middle of talking to a table about their complaint. The server would come by to drop off the food. As I was talking to the guests and the server was placing the food down, Travis would come by the table and remove the plate of a certain guest. I had no idea that Travis and that guest already had an altercation and he told them they could not eat here. He should've told the server prior to them taking the order as well as reinforced it with the guest prior to them ordering. His belief was that he already told them they were not going to eat here, and they should've left. He would purposely let them order and allow the food to come to the table so that he could remove it in front of them. He wanted to make a point to them that he was running things and not them. I would be just standing there in awe.

The guest would look at me and say, "Aren't you a manager? Why are you allowing him to take our food away like this?" I would just inform them that it was not my call and that he already made the decision. The guest would say, "So I just got to sit here with no food while the rest of my party eat?" Travis would advise them that he already told them they would not be eating here, and his decision was final.

Travis repeated acts like this all the time. Although he knew everything there was to know about the restaurant, he should've still been with the FBI. He needed that kind of structure and the chain of command that could keep him in check. Kassaundra was very much in control of the restaurant, but she couldn't control Travis.

Travis never nixed words when we were in manager meetings. If he didn't agree with Kassaundra, he would say so. He wouldn't agree just to agree. He also never nixed words with Franklin either. Although him and Franklin somehow got along, he rarely agreed with anything he said. I felt bad for Kassaundra; she had two managers in Franklin and Travis that were hard to manage. She also had Momma, who was hard to manage because she didn't care about anything. Momma wasn't going to fight too hard about anything with the guests or the crew. She was only there to swipe her card, lock the door, and get a paycheck. And then there was me. I knew how to talk to guests, but that was about it. I was brand new to management and they sent me to this rough restaurant. I was over my head and I think Kassaundra knew it.

Over the next few weeks, Travis and I worked quite a few shifts together. He had his style and I had my style. Although we had different styles, we still wanted the same thing: a professional and smooth-running operation. We would end up working well together. He was no-nonsense and I was trying to learn from him on how to be stern.

LUCAS

As a manager, we were not supposed to fire anyone. We were supposed to document them, send them home, and let the GM make the final decision on if they were going to get terminated. This would work with most of the managers, but if Travis sent you home, you were not coming back.

On one Friday night, I witnessed Travis fire someone. It was a server named Lucas. Lucas was not a good server and he continued to mess up every shift he worked. This night, Lucas was out of control. He was taking at least ten minutes to get to his table after they were seated, and they wouldn't see him for another ten minutes afterward. The guests would now be at their tables, seated for at least twenty minutes without water or bread. When he finally would come back to the tables, he would offer no apology or even act concerned.

To make matters worse, not only was he taking too long, but he was also forgetting to put the orders into the computer. He kept coming back to the kitchen asking for his order. Repeatedly, the line cooks would tell him they didn't have a ticket for him. Lucas would start yelling and swearing at the cooks. I told the guy to calm down. This happened at least four different times. Each time, Travis had to go talk to his tables. Lucas would swear up and down that he put the order in, but he hadn't. Travis was getting upset about this and tried talking to Lucas.

"Lucas, this is the fourth time that I went to your table because of your untimely service. Each time, you forgot to put the order in as well," Travis would calmly state.

"Man, I didn't forget to put the damn order in. Your kitchen fuckin up is what the problem is," Lucas shouted.

Travis would pause and try to contain himself. "Lucas, calm down and don't talk to me like that," Travis responded.

"I ain't got to calm down. Your kitchen fucking up and I'm losing tips because of that. I can't wait to tell Kassaundra how horrible this shift is," Lucas retorted.

After the guy continued to yell and would not contain himself, Travis told him, "You know what, you can tell Kassaundra tomorrow, because you are done for the day. I am transferring your tables over to another server and you can go home!"

Lucas became irate and uncontrollable after that. He knocked over some of the trays in the kitchen and continued to yell as he walked toward Travis. He looked like he was on drugs. This did not faze Travis one bit. I think he welcomed this.

Travis swiftly moved closer to him and got an inch from his face. Now Travis looked deranged and out of control. I was afraid that Travis was about to pummel Lucas, but Travis quickly regained his composure. He smiled at Lucas but stayed in his face. "Lucas, give me your check presenter and leave this building now." Travis grimaced.

Lucas did hand it over but started to swear at Travis as he walked away. Travis smiled at him, not concerned at all at his behavior. Travis told him once again to leave the building and that he was not to come back anymore. Suddenly, Lucas seemed to snap out of his stupor as he advised Travis that he had to work tomorrow and was supposed to be talking to Kassaundra.

Travis looked at him and said, "Don't worry about coming in tomorrow, you don't work here anymore. Now please leave!" The server looked as if he wanted to challenge Travis, but he thought better about it and just left.

The next day, both myself and Travis had to close. When we came in to work, Lucas was in the office talking to Kassaundra. He was pleading for his job back. Kassaundra asked for both me and Travis to come into the office with them. This guy was acting as if he were a saint. When both Travis and I told our side of the story, Lucas stated that we were both lying. Travis had saved the receipts from the day before that he had to compensate to the guests for the repeated mistakes. He presented the receipts to Kassaundra while grinning at Lucas. While Travis explained the compensations to Kassaundra, Lucas became irate and started swearing. Kassaundra told him that he must calm down at once. The guy started acting deranged again. We could instantly tell that something was wrong with him. Kassaundra told Lucas that she was going to stick with Travis's recommendation that he be terminated. The guy still wanted to get loud and out of control but he looked at Travis who seemed as if he was ready to kill him. Lucas just shook his head and left.

Later that night, Lucas came back in and sat at our bar. At first, we didn't think nothing of it. He was no longer employed with us. As long as he paid for his drink and food, he was no bother to us. However, as Travis and I were both in the kitchen, the bartender came rushing in telling us that we need to go talk to this table immediately. We both instinctively knew that it had something to do with Lucas. I hurried and left the kitchen to go to the table. Travis was a few steps behind me as well. As I went to the table, Travis fell back and conversed with the bartender to find out more.

There were two young women sitting there, looking irritated. As I introduced myself to them, they interrupted. "Are you the manager?" they demanded.

I said, "Yes, I am. How can I help you ladies?"

"We've been violated by that guy sitting at your bar!" one of the ladies exclaimed.

I looked and saw Lucas sitting at the end of the bar. I asked them what had occurred.

They said, "Just look, he is doing it now!"

I thought they were exaggerating, but what I saw next I wasn't prepared for.

Lucas was sitting at the end of the bar looking right at the girls. He was jacking off as he was looking at them. The position he was sitting at the bar hid him enough from the rest of the dining room that they hadn't seen what he was doing. However, the two ladies could see everything. Lucas never attempt to put his penis away. It was like he was in a trance.

On cue, I saw Travis walking swiftly toward him. He had seen this as well. I thought Travis was going to pick this guy up and throw him out of the window. Travis walked up to the guy's other side (opposite of where his penis was out) and told him to get out of this restaurant immediately. He advised him that if we ever saw him again, he would have him arrested. The guy scurried up and ran out of the restaurant. His pants were still falling as he ran out of the restaurant.

I was in disbelief. I had never seen anything like this in my life. We apologized to the two young ladies and bought their entire meal. We never did tell them this guy used to work here. I was glad to know that I was never going to see Lucas ever again. I needed a strong drink after that night.

Unfortunately, the next day, Lucas came in during lunch. It was, once again, me and Travis working. As soon as we saw him, we completely ignored him and called the police. Travis and I purposely didn't go speak with him. We didn't want to spook him and make him leave. We wanted the police to deal with him. Fortunately for us, the police didn't take long at all to get there. As soon as the police walked in, Travis and I walked up to the bar. Lucas had not seen the police yet. Travis told him that he needed to leave and never enter this building again. Travis was more menacing than the previous night.

Lucas didn't seem fazed and looked as if he was ready for an altercation. Travis walked away and, for a moment, Lucas thought he won. He snickered as he saw Travis retreat. As Travis was walking away, the police were walking toward the guy. Lucas never saw them coming. He almost jumped out of his seat when the police approached him. The police were putting their gloves on as they approached him. We had already advised the 911 dispatcher of the prior actions and the police were unsure of what they were dealing with. Lucas tried to talk himself out of the arrest, but the police wanted to hear nothing of it. They slapped the handcuffs on him and took him away. We would never see him again!

THAT AIN'T MINE

As if this day was not already unbelievable that wasn't the only distraction we were going to have for the day. After things settled down with Lucas getting arrested, I went and started managing the kitchen and Travis went back to managing the dining room. Things were going well until someone told me that Travis needed my help with something in the dining room. I went out to the dining room and didn't see him anywhere in sight. I finally saw him kneeling on one knee talking to a table. He was talking to them quietly and they were laughing. Once he saw me, he waved me over.

"Hey, Carter, come here please."

At first, I thought these were his friends and he wanted to introduce me. I approached the table and he handed me something in a plastic bag.

Travis looked at me and said, "Don't look at this in the dining room. Why don't you take it to the manager's office and then look at it?"

I was confused on what this was, but I didn't open my hand until I reached the kitchen. I opened my hand up and looked at the bag and instantly knew what it was. I quickly closed my hand back up and went to the office. As I entered the office and closed the door, I put the bag on our desk and looked at it. Yep, it was a bag of marijuana. I was so confused on why Travis would give this to me. Did he think that we were cool enough that he could give something like this to me? Were these his friends at the table that gave this to him? A million questions were going through my head. I was upset with him for involving me with this. He had struck me as being a professional and character-driven guy. As I pondered, Travis came into the office.

I immediately asked him, "Why did you give this to me?"

Surprised, he looked at me and said, "You don't think that was mine, do you?"

I didn't say a word, but just looked at him.

"Look, dude, I was walking by that section when these guests stopped me. The guests told me their server just dropped that bag of marijuana on the floor and hadn't noticed. They explained that as the server was taking their order book out of their front apron pocket, the bag of marijuana fell out. The funny thing is that the four tables in that area saw the marijuana fall out of her apron, but she hadn't noticed that she dropped it," he explained.

Travis told me that he ended up buying food for all four tables. He didn't want them calling our corporate office about this.

I was in disbelief about how this day was going so far. Travis advised me that he had already told Simone to not seat the server anymore. The server had no idea what was going on. Travis had told her that she was cut (meaning that she could leave for the day). She was elated that she was getting off so early on a Saturday. Travis wanted her to finish cleaning her section and side work before we spoke to her about what happened. Travis stated that it made no sense for us to clean her section. Let her do the dirty work and then we would fire her!

Once she was done with her section and had given all her money to the Blue Crab, Travis asked her to come into the office. She said sure! She had no idea that she had even lost the marijuana. I wondered how much she had on her for her not to even notice that the bag was missing. We left the bag sitting on the office desk. As she entered the office, we closed the door behind her. This is when she saw the marijuana, but she tried to act as if she didn't notice it.

Travis asked, "Do you know what that bag is?"

Acting surprised, she looked at us in shock and said, "Why do you all have a bag of weed on your desk?"

Travis said, "We should be asking you this. This came from you!"

As innocently as possible, she stated, "That ain't mine. I don't smoke that stuff."

Travis explained to her that several guests saw the marijuana fall from her apron.

She excessively denied this was hers.

"Let us see your apron, please!" Travis demanded.

She didn't want to give it to us. She took it off and then changed her mind. "Um, no sir, I don't want to give you my apron," she stated. "This is my apron and you don't have the right to look inside it. I have some female personal hygiene items in the pockets, and I shouldn't have to show that to you."

We both knew that she was lying. Travis advised her that the apron was property of the Blue Crab and we could inspect this at any time. She refused to give up her apron. Travis advised her that she could come in and talk to Kassaundra about her job, but that she is suspended and would be fired! She said nothing as she grabbed her apron and walked out. I knew that she wasn't going to forget the apron. She must've had quite a few more bags of marijuana in it.

Later in the day, once the rest of the crew found out about what happened to her, they all started to spill the beans. It started coming out that she was selling weed to both the customers and the crew! She had some balls to sell weed to the customers. To further my shock, she came in to talk to Kassaundra later that night. She said that she didn't drop that bag and that Travis and I were both lying and trying to set her up. Kassaundra didn't buy a word of what she was saying. She told her that she was fired! Thank God!

THE WHISTLE BLOWER

As the weeks passed, Kasssaundra started allowing me to work some shifts on my own. In other words, she wasn't babysitting me any longer. If I worked during the daytime, I would still work with another manager, but at night I would be on my own. I understood why I wasn't working on my own during the day shift. You had to check in deliveries, do invoices, orders, etc. I wasn't quite ready to do any of those things. I also didn't want to make a mistake.

Although I was good enough to work by myself, I still didn't garner the respect that the other managers had gained. I wasn't too much older than most of the servers that I was managing, and everyone that worked in the kitchen was older than me. It didn't help that I had no idea what I was doing in the kitchen. It was hard to manage people that knew the job better than you. I hadn't mastered the art of fake-it-till-you-make-it yet.

By the way, this was a much different crew than I was used to. I had never worked at a Blue Crab location that was so tough. I'm not sure who was tougher: the guests or the crew. This crew was inappropriate and unprofessional. I guess this was a byproduct of who the leader of this restaurant was. It also didn't help that they worked with Franklin and Momma mostly on night shifts. Nothing bothered Franklin too much and he liked bending the rules. And Momma just didn't care about anything. They were a hard act to follow.

On one occasion, I had just gotten in to work. It was slightly after three o'clock p.m. I went around and said my hellos to the crew. Franklin was the opening manager for that day, and everyone was in a playful mood and too loud. He was sitting in the anchor eating when I came in. He was having just as much fun as the crew and he was for sure louder than them. I said hello to him and went back up front. I went by the host podium and talked to Jack. He was upset because the restaurant was dirty. He complained that everyone was playing and acting silly, but no one was bussing their tables. He pointed at the servers who were standing by the end of the bar. I told him that I would get everyone together and that we would get this restaurant cleaned up.

While I was talking to Jack, out of nowhere, I heard a loud screeching sound like a whistle. It was coming from where our servers were all standing around. I looked up at them and signaled for them to cut it out. I did this discreetly because some guests were walking in the front doors at the same time. After I said hello to the guests, I heard the whistle blow out again. Now, everyone in the restaurant was looking around trying to figure out who was blowing the whistle. I beelined over to where the servers were congregated.

"Hey! Which of you is blowing this whistle?" I demanded.

They admitted they heard the whistle, but it was not them.

I knew someone was lying to me. "I'm just being straight with you, if someone blows this whistle again, I will find out and this will be your last day with the Blue Crab."

They all laughed and said, "We really don't know who it was."

I just knew they were lying to me. I reiterated that someone needed to give over this whistle before someone got fired. They again stated they didn't know who was blowing it. I was just about to walk off when I heard the whistle again. This time, someone blew the whistle for about ten seconds. To my surprise, I whipped around and saw that it was one of our customers sitting at the bar. I immediately started in their direction. One of the servers shouted out, "Yeah, go get 'em." I just shook my head.

The guest was a large lady with her even larger husband. I was so agitated that I never introduced myself or gave my title when I approached them. "Hello, ma'am, could you please not blow your whistle in the restaurant again?" I asked politely.

"Who are you?" she asked.

"I'm Carter, and I'm the manager here."

She replied, "Yes, I'm Bev and this is my husband Phil." I was about to interject, but she interrupted. She held up her whistle and said, "Oh, and this is Sheila." She informed me that Shelia was her whistle and that if she wanted to blow it, then she would.

"Ma'am, I have to ask you to please not blow that whistle again."

She looked at me and placed the whistle back up to her lips and blew it loudly right in my face. I was furious but maintained my composure. I attempted to talk again, but each time I attempted, she would blow the whistle in my face. Finally, she stopped blowing the whistle and her husband decided to talk to me.

"Look, man, you just need to walk away from us!"

Not doing such a great job at holding my composure, I told them they needed to leave the restaurant immediately.

"Look, man, like I told you before, you just need to walk away," he retorted.

I advised him that if they didn't leave, I would call the police on them.

The husband grinned at me and said, "I don't feel that well. My stomach hurts. Must've been something that I ate here. You should really walk away before I throw up on you."

I indeed walked away. I walked straight to the phone to call the police. While I was on the phone with the police, they got up to leave. The guests advised me as they walked past me, while I was on the phone with the authorities, that they weren't going to pay the bill.

Unfortunately, they left the parking lot before the police got there. I was disappointed, but I did remember their faces. If I ever saw them at the restaurant again, I would ensure they would never be served.

The crew saw how upset that I was, and they started laughing at me. They said that I should've went and got Franklin to handle that. I was mad at them for laughing at me. However, they were probably correct. It was confirmed they were correct because when I saw Franklin, he said, "Who the fuck was blowing a whistle?" I just shook my head, but the crew was right. I should've got the loud and disrespectful manager to deal with the loud and disrespectful guests.

WHAT IS YOUR MISSION STATEMENT

As I continued to work shifts by myself, the shifts continued to get worse and worse. The problem was that I was working with the dinner shift crew and they were horrible. Most of the tenured and experienced employees worked during the day. and the inexperienced and problematic crew worked at night. Things would usually go fine from 3:00 p.m. to about 7:00 p.m. This restaurant would not get busy until late in the evening. Once it picked up, things would go to hell.

For a while, I thought that our line cooks were the slowest cooks in America. The food always took too long to come out. The servers would be getting on the cooks' nerves with the constant complaining about how long the food was taking. As I observed them, I noticed they weren't moving with a sense of urgency. It drove me bananas that I was not good enough to help. All the managers except for Momma were good in the kitchen. Kassaundra was better than any of them on the line and Franklin wasn't too far behind. Travis was also good at jumping in to help. I never saw Momma do anything in the kitchen, and all I could do was work the fry station.

I would eventually start helping in the kitchen at night. Like clockwork, every night around 7:00 p.m., I would grab an apron and go to the fry station. I hated doing this because there would be no manager coverage in the front. After a few days of working on the line, I realized that our cooks were not as bad as I thought. The problem was, they never had product to cook. We were always waiting for food to be made. As mentioned earlier, we typically would have Simone's beau, Jeremiah, working evening prep. Although he came in at 4:00 p.m., he would never start working until around 6:00 p.m. By this time, we would be out of a lot of items. The morning prep people would leave as soon as he got in. They used to stay and help for a while, but they were upset that he was practically getting paid to not work for two hours while they did the work.

One evening, food was taking a long time to come out. I couldn't afford to help them because we were understaffed in the dining room. A lot of guests were complaining as were the servers. For about a straight hour, I was getting called to one table after the next.

One table gave me a real hard time. This gentleman pointed out everything that was wrong with the restaurant. He told me that he could tell we were understaffed. He told me to look at our floors and our tables. The floors were dirty and most of the tables weren't pre-bussed at all. "Young man, this is the result of poor management! I am embarrassed to even be in this restaurant and, furthermore, I am embarrassed for you. Does the Blue Crab even have a mission statement?"

I said that we did indeed have a mission statement.

He asked if I knew what the mission statement was.

I said that I did.

"Could you tell me what the mission statement is?" he asked.

I said, "Pardon me?"

"You heard me; I would like you to tell me what your mission statement is."

He saw my hesitation and said that he could just call my corporate office and have them tell me what it was. I wanted to punch this guy in the throat for talking to me like that. However, I was so afraid of someone calling the corporate office on me. If they contacted the corporate office, then our director, Chris, would be notified. I didn't want to risk losing my job for having a guest complaint.

Before I could think about what I was doing, I stood up straight and recited,

"THE BLUE CRAB WANTS TO BE YOUR CHOICE FOR EVERYDAY DINING. WE GUARANTEE THAT YOU WILL RECEIVE TOP OF THE LINE FOOD AND SERVICE. OUR FOOD WILL BE FRESH, HOT, AND TASTY. OUR SERVICE WILL BE EXCELLENT AND BEYOND MEASURE. THIS AGAIN IS OUR GUARANTEE TO YOU."

As I finished up, the customer asked, "Now, do you truly believe this statement?"

I told him that I did believe in it.

He started in on me again, questioning me. "Well, if you do believe in this statement, why didn't we receive hot food and excellent service?"

I began to answer his question, but he interrupted.

"I don't need an answer, just think about it. The next time that I come in, I expect to see this restaurant living up to this expectation." He then stated, "Since our service wasn't excellent and beyond measure, we shouldn't be paying for our meal." I agreed with him and took care of their entire meal.

I didn't do it because he was asking me to but because it was the right thing to do. We had dropped the ball and didn't serve hot food or give great service. He was pleased with my decision and was full of himself. He then went a little further and asked for a gift card for the next time. I told him that I couldn't do anything else for them. For whatever reason, I snapped out of my foolishness. I was so afraid to have someone call the corporate office that I let them degrade me in this manner. I became upset with myself for selling myself out! I excused myself from the table because I wanted to hit him for talking to me like that.

Walking away from the table, I saw Maria at a table wiping it down. She had heard everything. She was laughing at me uncontrollably. Once I walked in the kitchen, she was on my heels repeating the mission statement. For the remainder of the night, she teased me about this! Although I was embarrassed, it was a little funny. I vowed that I would never let someone demean me like I allowed this customer to.

Maria's Place

After several weeks of working night shifts, I started to get the hang of things. Now things weren't perfect, but it was better. I had started to complain to Kassaundra about Jeremiah not doing anything for the first few hours and that it was putting us behind. He was too busy following behind Simone. If he wasn't talking to Simone, he was talking to Maria. At first I thought he was dating Maria as well, but then I heard him call her *big sis* on several occasions. Although he showed no urgency to do anything for anyone, he would go out his way to do anything Maria needed.

Kassaundra sat down with Jeremiah, but of course Jeremiah disagreed. Nothing changed with his performance, but Kassaundra did start putting someone else to work with me at nights. She put a shift lead with me.

Now, each of the Blue Crabs had shift leads. A shift lead was not quite a manager but was an employee that wanted to go into management. The shift lead would assist management on a shift when there was only one manager working. We had two shift leads that worked here. The first one was the guy who asked me for five dollars on my first shift and the second was an older lady named Hazel. I had met Hazel already and had no idea that she was a shift lead. Hazel was old enough to be my mom. Matter of fact, she had two daughters that were my age.

Hazel was a bartender that could hardly keep up at the bar. On one of my first shifts, I went to get change from her drawer, and she stopped me immediately. She advised me that no one could go into her drawer and that included managers. I was like, *Here we go again. Another bitchy woman that works here.* I had to tell her that I was a manager and I was not about to ask for permission to get change from her. I tried to be as respectful as I could be, but I didn't want to take any crap from her either. The next thing you know, she was crying and speaking to Franklin and Kassaundra in the office about me. This was the moment I found out she was a shift lead. She was stating to Kassaundra that none of the managers ever listened to her or treated her as a manager. The only one that showed her respect was Maria.

I was confused about why she would say Maria's name while referring to managers.

Franklin butted in and said, "Um, girl, you know that you aren't a manager, right?"

I almost laughed out loud, but I concealed my laughter.

Kassaundra asked me and Franklin to both leave the office while she spoke with Hazel. After we got far enough away from the office, Franklin looked at me and said, "Can you believe that bitch really thinks she's a manager? Kassaundra be babying her, but I have to check that bitch all the time."

I asked Franklin, "Why did she reference Maria when talking about the managers?"

"Oh, because she's scared of Maria. She tried telling Maria what to do a few times, and Maria tore her ass apart. Now Hazel may try to manage other people, but she never wants any part of Maria."

* * *

Hazel was the shift lead that I worked most of my nights with at the beginning. She was okay despite our few run-ins, but she really thought that she was in charge. She was a little too much, however. The crew respected her for her age but nothing else. She would always get upset and then start crying if things didn't go her way. I almost wanted to go back to working by myself.

On one evening, we were working together and she asked if she could work in the kitchen. Normally she wanted to work out front. I was okay with her working the kitchen. I was tired of being in there every night anyhow. Plus, Jeremiah wasn't working tonight (of course, Simone was off), so we should've had enough food. It should have been a relatively easy night for Hazel in the kitchen. The shift started good despite Simone not being our hostess.

Since neither Jack nor Simone was working, we had another host named Axel working. Axel was different than Simone. Axel had another job and would come straight from his other job to the Blue Crab. Axel was a cool guy but not personable at all, unlike Simone.

He was woman-crazy as well, despite him being an older gentleman. He could hardly focus if a nice-looking woman walked by. He never tried to hide it if a nice-looking woman with an equally nice butt walked by. He would almost run into the wall looking at them. The word from everyone was that he had a huge crush on Maria. He could never concentrate when she was at work.

Now you couldn't find a harder worker than Axel, but he needed to be refined. Axel was a host as well as a busser on the weekend. He needed to just be a busser. He was not personable with the guests and he walked too fast. Axel would always be sweating because he was doing too much. Also, just like Maria, I think he stayed drunk.

Axel used any opportunity to work out. When he bussed tables, he would stack everything onto five trays to make it heavy. He would do arm curls with the trays as he walked through the dining room headed to the kitchen. I even caught him doing triceps dips in the lobby using the bench that guests sit on. How ridiculous! I told him to cut that out immediately. I also had to tell him to slow down in his walking when he was seating tables. He would be ten steps ahead of guests when walking them to the table. The guests had to keep up with him.

Any woman could tell him anything and he would abide, but he had an extreme low tolerance for men getting loud with him. Although Axel was a kind person, he was always ready for an altercation with a guy. I had to teach him how to calm down.

I had my work cut out for me with Axel working out front and Crying-Ass Hazel working in the kitchen. The night started off slow. It stayed like this until six o'clock. We started to pick up in volume and had to go on a slight wait list. Of course, Maria was late, and she had two tables that had been waiting for her for fifteen minutes prior to six o'clock. Axel had told them Maria would be in at six o'clock. She didn't arrive until almost six thirty. We now had ten parties waiting to be seated. People were starting to get uneasy. The good thing is that we had two other servers scheduled to come in at six thirty. After Maria and the other two servers got settled in, Axel started seating guests. We were able to get off wait quickly and things started to smooth out.

Although being off wait, some of the other servers started complaining they didn't have enough tables. Two of the servers stated that they only had one table each. How was this even possible when we were just on a wait? One server, Beverly, was angry and said the host gave Maria most of the tables and this wasn't fair.

I went to Axel and asked him how many tables Maria had.

"Boss, she has eight tables."

I was beside myself. I asked Axel, "Why would you give anyone that many tables?"

He stated that Maria told him to give her all the tables waiting and that is what he did.

I told him this made no sense at all. The most tables that anyone else had was four and the two other servers who came in at six thirty only had one table apiece. Why in the world he would give Maria eight was beyond me. I told him to not seat Maria or anyone else that many tables again. I went over to Maria's section and three of the tables were still sitting there with their menus pushed to the side, which indicated they were ready to order. One of the tables was a party of seven. That party stopped me and said that no server had been by and they'd been sitting there for almost fifteen minutes. They were upset they already had to wait in the lobby for thirty minutes and we were slow, and now here was another fifteen minutes and they still didn't have a server. I apologized and told them a server would be over immediately.

I decided that I was going to give these other three tables away to people who didn't have but one table. I gave the first two tables away quickly and then I asked Beverly, since she only had one table and was the most experienced, to take the party of seven. She seemed a little reluctant to take the party of seven. Now, I was surprised because she was the one complaining about having only one table.

As I made it back to the kitchen, I overheard Beverly asking Maria if she was cool if she took that table.

"Girl, you don't have to take that table. I got it, they will just have to wait," Maria replied.

I interjected, "Beverly, please go ahead and take this table. Maria already has too many tables as is. This party of seven is already unhappy and I don't want them to wait any further."

Maria completely disregarded my comment. She said, "Beverly, like I said, don't worry about the table, I got it. They are just going to have to wait!"

Hazel even jumped in and told me that Maria could handle it and that she could take the table. I was starting to lose my cool. I grunted, "Beverly, please get to the table immediately." Beverly looked at Maria and Hazel as if to get approval.

I looked at them all and said, "This is not a request! I made my decision and I'm not going to discuss it any further." Beverly finally got the picture and headed to the dining room to take the table.

Maria became hostile. She told me, "You are fucking up my money! Since you aren't letting me do my job, I am going home."

I told her that we were busy and that she was not going home. Hazel tried to talk to me in front of the crew and I told her my decision was final. I went back out to the dining room and composed myself. I wasn't sure what was worse: that Hazel wanted to confront me about Maria or that Maria had the audacity to tell me that I was fucking up her money.

The next hour went smoothly. I avoided talking to both Maria and Hazel. I did overhear Maria tell someone, "He must not know that I run this place!" I started to interject but I just let it go. I made my point and I didn't care what she had to say.

I went back into the dining room and talked to a lot of tables. They said that everything was good. The party of seven even stated that we had redeemed ourselves from the earlier debacle. I noticed that a lot of tables were starting to get up, including Maria's. However, we were back on a wait. Two of Maria's tables were clean and ready to be sat, but Axel wasn't seating them. I went and told Axel to seat Maria.

He looked at me and stated, "Boss, Maria told me that she was cut" (meaning a manager told her she was done and could go home).

I was beside myself that she would tell him that. He looked conflicted and told me, "I can't seat her, boss, because she is cut."

"Axel, I did not cut Maria. I don't know why she told you this, but please continue to seat her."

I went back to the dining room and talked to a few more tables. I finally saw Axel come to Maria's section. I was satisfied that we were going to get off the wait, but Axel continued walking the guests past her section to another server's section. I thought maybe the other server was next in the seating rotation, so I gave it no further thought. However, I observed him continue to skip Maria's section and go to other tables, and we were still on a wait. I finally went to the front host podium and confronted Axel.

I asked, "Why are we still on a wait, but you still haven't sat Maria?"

He said, "Look, man, she told me she was cut. That's between the two of you. I don't want to get in the middle of y'all's disagreement."

Once again, I was beside myself. I looked at Axel and stated, "Axel, I am the manager, not Maria. If I must ask you to seat her again, you will not be working here anymore! I will not talk to you about this again. Now, do we understand each other?" He looked shocked but nodded that he understood.

When the next table came in, he looked reluctant, but he did seat her. After a few minutes, I noticed that Maria didn't stop by the table. I went into the kitchen and told her that she had been sat.

She laughed and said, "Naw, that's impossible, because I am cut. That must be your table!"

I replied, "No, Maria, that is not my table and I have not cut you. You need to get to that table. Unless you quit. You must've quit if you are refusing a table."

Of course, she had a rebuttal. "Naw, I didn't quit, and I still won't be going to that table or any other table. What I am going to do is go home and come back tomorrow. Hopefully, a real manager will be working."

Everyone in the kitchen was in awe. It was like they were in a tennis match as they were looking back and forth as myself and Maria continued our unnecessary disagreement. It took everything for me to not use profanity toward her. I kept my composure, however.

I went and started the table's order and since Maria refused to go to any new tables, I transferred her other two remaining tables over to me. Once Maria found out that I transferred the two tables to myself, she was furious. She demanded that I transfer them back. I told her that she needed to go home.

A few minutes later, Hazel came to me and said that Kassaundra was on the phone for me. I got to the phone and she asked me what happened between me and Maria. She also asked me why Hazel was crying. How did she know about any of this? And why was Hazel crying? I told her what happened and then she asked to speak back to Maria. Speak back to her! That meant that she had already spoken to Kassaundra first.

I went and got Maria and told her that Kassaundra was on the phone for her. I was quite satisfied that after Kassaundra found out that she refused to take a table that she would be done with her. For the next fifteen minutes, Kassaundra would have me, Hazel, and Maria coming back and forth to the phone to talk to her. Finally, she told me to transfer the two tables back to Maria and just let her go home. She told me that she would deal with this tomorrow. I was dissatisfied with her solution, but I was hoping that when Kassaundra said she would deal with this tomorrow, that it would result in the termination of Maria's employment.

Finally, Maria left the building, but Hazel would have nothing to say to me for the rest of the night. I told her crying ass that she could leave early if she wanted to. She took me up on the offer. Good riddance! Some of the crew were happy with me for the decision I made, and I was happy about that as well. Maria was a handful, but after today I doubted she would be working for the Blue Crab. The fact that she thought she could act like this and get away with it was unacceptable.

The next day, I wasn't scheduled to come in to work until three o'clock. However, Kassaundra called me early in the morning and asked if I could come in at noon. She wanted to sit down with me and Maria and go over last night's events. I didn't want to go in early, but I was elated to go in and sit down with Maria so that we could terminate her.

As soon as I walked into work, I noticed that Maria was

already there. Poor, stupid girl was already in her uniform. She could've just worn regular clothes to get terminated. I went to the office and told Kassaundra I was here. She told me to go sit down in the anchor and she would be right there. I went to the anchor and joyfully waited.

A few minutes later, Kassaundra came walking in with Maria. Maria sat down across from me and Kassaundra pulled up a chair and sat at the end of the table. Maria was staring at me like she wanted to claw my face off. I sat there and looked right back at her, laughing on the inside. We looked like two boxers after the prefight weigh-in. Kassaundra had some papers with her. I was getting anxious because I knew these were Maria's termination papers. I couldn't breathe, I was so excited.

Kassaundra asked Maria to give her side of the story. Maria was loud and over exaggerated everything as she told her side of the story. She pointed her fingers in my face and tried her best to belittle me. I let her tell her side without interrupting.

After she finished with her elaborate story, I told Kassaundra what occurred. I kept it short and sweet, just like this termination was about to be. I even told Kassaundra about her saying that I was "Fucking up her money" and that I wasn't a real manager.

Maria jumped in and said, "Well, you aren't really a real manager."

Kassaundra told her to quiet down and let me finish. I told her that I had nothing else to say. I was just waiting for her to flip over the termination papers, fire Maria. and let me get on with my day.

What happened next floored me. Instead of this being a termination letter, it was a piece of paper with Maria's name on the top left and my name on the top right. Kassaundra had it categorized as things Maria could've done better and things Carter could've done better. She asked Maria what her thoughts were about yesterday and what she would have done differently.

She said, "The only thing that I would've done differently is not to come to work, especially since a real manager wasn't working."

Without chastising her or anything, Kassaundra just looked at me and said, "What could you have done differently?" I was furious and at a loss of words. Kassaundra was going to let this chick get away with this nasty behavior. I couldn't say anything and just looked at them both. I was done. I looked at Kassaundra and said that I had nothing to say.

Kassaundra said that she would revisit this with us again and that she hoped we could figure out a way to work together. She then told Maria that she could work this morning since she missed out on money the night before. I was once again floored. So, this *bitch* gets to curse at a manager, make up her own rules, refuse to follow a manager's instructions, and nothing happens to her. And she gets to come in earlier and work since she missed out last night. This was pre-planned. That's why she had on her uniform. She and Kassaundra had already spoken prior to our conversation. No matter what I said, the outcome was going to be the same. I was confused on who was the general manager: Maria or Kassaundra! I felt disrespected. Damn, maybe it was true. Maria really did run this place!

I didn't have anything to say to Maria for about a month. She also never said anything to me. I was good with that. I didn't care if she was late, if she was drunk. or if she didn't show up to work. If Kassaundra didn't care, then I didn't care.

IGNORING THE CALL

Unfortunately, the horrible encounter I had with Maria wouldn't be the last time I had an altercation with a team member and Kassaundra didn't back me up. We had a cook named Tom that Kassaundra absolutely loved. Tom could do nothing wrong in her eyes.

Tom was a constant complainer and troublemaker. His constant complaints would trigger other cooks to complain as well. But don't get me wrong, Tom was the biggest issue.

Tom didn't want to follow directions, didn't really cook all that well, and would constantly leave his area, putting his fellow team members behind. Tom also liked to argue with the managers including Kassaundra and Travis. Kassaundra seemed to enjoy the arguing, however. She stated that Tom always argued because he was passionate about the business. I highly disagreed and thought Tom was not adding any value.

I complained to Kassaundra about both Tom and Gary quite often. Kassaundra agreed they both complained a lot but thought that besides Jasmine, Tom was our strongest cook. I said that Gary was possibly the strongest cook but not Tom. I also told Kassaundra that it didn't matter if they are strong cooks if they were bringing a negative culture. Kassaundra completely disagreed with me and stated that we would be in trouble without these guys.

Anyhow, one evening I was working, and everything was going wrong. Tom was the main cook this night and I was getting complaints the entire evening about the food. What made it worse was that every time that I went into the kitchen, he was yelling at people or getting into an argument. I tried to calm him down, but he was the type of guy that loved chaos. I even went on the line to try to help them.

Once I came onto the line, he started working even less and complaining more. I was able to make a phone call and get another cook in to help them out, but Tom still wouldn't stop complaining or starting arguments with people. I continued to try to help and calm him down, but eventually I was needed out front to talk to a guest.

Of course, the guest wanted to complain about the food. They stated the food not only took too long, but it was not presentable either. I apologized and asked if they would like for me to have their food remade. They told me they didn't have time for a recook and they just wanted the food to be taken off their bill. Thank God, because I really didn't want to have it remade. I didn't think that it was going to come back out looking any better.

One of our other cooks, Angie, was off work that day but happened to be at our bar drinking. Now, Angie was one of Franklin's best friends. They hung out together drinking all the time. Matter of fact, I was surprised that she was at our bar and not somewhere drinking with Franklin. When I walked past Angie, I heard our bartender complaining to her how awful tonight was and that Tom was in the kitchen cursing out everyone. I jokingly (halfheartedly) asked Angie if she wanted to come in the kitchen and help out. Angie said, "Sure, but I'm on my second Long Island!" I really wished she hadn't been drinking because I would have done anything to get another cook on the line.

Now Angie wasn't the fastest cook either, but she was always in a good mood and she knew what she was doing. I had never seen Angie in a bad mood, but then again, she was friends with Franklin and Maria, which meant that she was probably drunk most of the time. I would probably be in a better mood if I had a drink before coming into this place, especially dealing with Tom and his foul behavior.

After realizing that I technically couldn't let Angie work due to her drinking before work, I reluctantly went back to the kitchen. Immediately upon entry, I could hear Tom going off on someone.

I went to the line and said, "Tom I really need you to calm down and stop talking to people like this."

Before I could say anything else, he interjected and said, "Sorry, I need to go to the bathroom."

He took his apron, hair net, and gloves off and walked off the line. The other guys that worked the line weren't main cooks, so they just patiently waited with no sense of urgency for Tom to come back and bark instructions at them. Meanwhile, tickets were backing up and myself or the line guys didn't know what to do. The servers were now angrier by the second and were looking at me for guidance.

I winged it and started my best at cooking what was necessary. One of the other line cooks (really, could you call them cooks?) commented that it was a shame that a manager didn't know what he was doing.

I quickly snapped back and stated, "What is worse: a new

manager that isn't strong or someone like you, who has been here for three years and still can't contribute? At least I'm trying to do something."

I realized that I was starting to lose my cool. I saw Maria in the kitchen trying to stir some stuff up as well. I was waiting for her to say something to me. I was ready for the fight.

It had been ten minutes and Tom finally came back to the line smelling like cigarettes. This is when I realized that he didn't have to go to the bathroom; he wanted to go catch a quick smoke. Once he walked on the line, he stopped and looked at what was going on and smirked. He looked at me and said, "Wow, you really fucked this up, didn't you?"

I was livid.

"Don't talk to me in this manner."

Once again, while I was talking to him, he walked away. Now, at this point, I felt like the rapper 2Pac: "All Eyez on Me"! As everyone was looking at me, like what was I going to do now, I started following Tom. He went into one of the prep coolers to cool off. I waited for him to come out and then I stated, "What did you just say to me?"

Tom wouldn't repeat what he said, but he walked up to me and got into my face. He was about an inch away from me and just stared at me. I felt like a confrontation was about to happen, so I told him that he needed to leave.

He said, "Hell naw, I'm not leaving!"

"Look, you can either leave this kitchen right now, or I can have the police come and make you leave this kitchen. Either way, you will be leaving this kitchen," I barked.

"So, you going to call the police on me. That's some bullshit! I'm going to call Kassaundra," Tom barked back.

He started walking out the kitchen, but he was sure to make a scene. He continued to curse as he removed his apron and tossed it on the floor. He next removed his disposable gloves and threw them on the floor and then his hair net.

I remained unmoved as he made his display. He finally turned around and exited the kitchen. Now, I wanted to curse and throw things also because I didn't know what I was doing on the line.

I started to head to the line, but instead I headed to the bar. Luckily, Angie was still at the bar, but she was now on her third Long Island. I didn't even care at this point. It was either lock the doors for the night or let a drunk cook come and work the line. I knew that we couldn't lock up early, so I elected to go with option two: the drunk cook.

"Hey, Angie, I know I asked you before, but we could really use you right now. Tom was acting like a fool and I had to send him home."

She said, "Dude, you know I'm on my third drink!"

I said, "I don't even care at this point. We need you! Have you paid for your drinks and food yet?"

"Um, no," she replied.

"Okay, great! I will take care of your bill and I will have the Blue Crab pay you forty bucks from our petty cash tonight if you could come cook these last two hours. I will even clock you in. Just come help bail us out," I begged.

She looked at me, downed the rest of her Long Island, and said, "I'm on the way!"

As she was on her way to the kitchen, I noticed Tom was still there. He was at our host podium on the phone talking to someone. He looked as if he wanted to kill me.

As soon as the crew saw Angie heading on the line, they

cheered. Maria even made the comment to another server, "This is the first real manager thing that I've seen him do." I heard her but chose to ignore her. I still came on the line and helped. Angie told me to go to the fry station and then she moved the other three cooks around to help push the food out faster. It took about thirty minutes for us to get caught back up, but eventually we did. I was able to get back off the line and Angie assured me that she had it under control. I was relieved but a little worried that I let her come on the line despite her being slightly drunk. However, the guest complaints about the food stopped.

Once I went back out to the dining room, I noticed that Tom was still sitting in the lobby. A few minutes later, the host came to me and said that Kassaundra was on the phone for me. *Here we go again.* I was not about to answer the call. I told her to tell Kassaundra that I was busy and that I would call her back. I was not about to go back and forth with Kassaundra on what I could've done better.

Over the next hour, Kassaundra continued to call, and I continued to ignore her calls. I was not about to go replay the same phone conversations we just had not too long ago with Maria. I'm pretty sure Tom told her that I was ignoring her calls because he was still sitting in the lobby pouting like a big kid.

About fifteen minutes prior to closing, Tom walked up to me and said, "Not sure if you know this, but Kassaundra is on the phone waiting to talk to you. She said that you need to come to the phone immediately."

I looked at Tom and said, "I didn't realize you were still here. You shouldn't be answering the phone. I told you to leave."

He grimaced at me and said, "So you aren't going to go to the phone when your boss told you to come to the phone?"

I replied, "So you aren't going to leave the restaurant when your boss told you to leave?"

"I'll be sure to let Kassaundra know that you are ignoring her phone call!"

I ignored him and went back to taking care of the restaurant. He just looked at me, smirked, and sat back down in the lobby.

Well, just after closing, much to my surprise, Kassaundra came bursting through the doors. She was furious and wanted to make sure that everyone, including me, knew it. She immediately started barking at everyone. She looked completely unprofessional as she had on her baseball cap and flip flops. Her shirt was way too small and showed her belly.

I had completely forgotten that we used to call her B.T. back in the day until this moment. Her small shirt couldn't contain her boobs. Her boobs were bouncing around all over the place and so was her stomach. It was quite unappealing, to say the least.

As soon as she saw me, she came marching up to me and barked, "Carter, did you not get the message that I had been calling up here for you for the last two hours?"

I told her that I was busy cooking and dealing with the guests and couldn't call her.

I was nervous and confused. I was nervous because I knew that I was wrong for not taking her phone call. I didn't want to get fired for this. But most importantly, I was confused. When she was yelling at me, I started shaking nervously and stuttering as I tried to respond to her. This had never happened to me before. I had never been afraid of anyone. Why was I nervous?

I shook that off quickly, because I could tell that she could sense I was nervous. I told her that I was busy because I had to send Tom home for being insubordinate. I also added that I told

Tom to leave the building and he refused. Kassaundra advised me that Tom had called her and made her aware of the situation. She said, "I was the one that told Tom not to leave and if you had come to the phone, then you would've known."

As if I weren't present, Kassaundra looked at Tom and told him to go in the back and help them clean up. Tom glided past me, grinning. She then looked at me and told me to let Angie know that she could go home. Once again, I was furious! I couldn't believe this woman continuously went with the crew over me!

Angie didn't mind leaving at all because she didn't want to do the cleaning up. As she was leaving, I heard Angie and Maria talking. Maria even said, "Wow, that is fucked up! How is Kassaundra going to bring Tom back in after he was acting a fool like that?" Even though I agreed with her, it was funny how she thought it was messed up, but when it was her acting this way, it was acceptable!

I later found out that Kassaundra paid Tom for his two hours of doing nothing. The time he sat in the lobby, refusing to leave, he was getting paid for it. I was done and didn't want anything to do with this crew. I decided that I was going to take the check and figure out how to get transferred out of this horrible location.

Mr. Bennett

Although I tried to stay to myself, I would end up having another altercation at work. We had an older male server named Mr. Bennett. Mr. Bennett was pretty much on the weird side. He was an extra-large and tall guy with a bald head, and he had a gray beard with matching gray sideburns. He seemed to be pleasant at first, but once you got into a conversation with him, you realized that he was weird. You would instantly try to get yourself out of the conversation as quickly as possible.

He would always redirect any conversation you were having to something having to deal with the planet or stars, the oceans or the rivers. People jokingly started calling him EWF after the old famous group of his time Earth, Wind & Fire. He was also a conspiracy theorist. He always thought that someone had something against him and was coming after him.

Although Mr. Bennett was a slow-paced server, his tables loved him. We had a lot of younger and not-so-professional servers and obviously Mr. Bennett was the opposite. He was articulate and descriptive when it came to the food. Every time a table would request him, he would question the host. He wanted to know who were they, how did they know him, did they ask for him by first and last name, had they eaten here before? We would tell Mr.

Bennett to calm down and just go and take the table. No one was looking for him in here. He would reply, "You never know what these people want—it could be someone from the government!" I would just shake my head at him. He was one strange dude!

One evening as I was about to leave, I had started going around to say goodbye to everyone. I had started the process of making sure every time I came in, before I got to work, I would go around and say hello to everyone, and I would also start doing this as I left everyday as well. I was happy to be leaving. Kassaundra had come in at noon and Travis came in at three. It was a little after six o'clock and Kassaundra said that I was good to go. So, I started the process of saying goodbye to everyone. I started off in the kitchen and then I made my way to the front of the house. Normally, I wouldn't stop and say goodbye to a server if they were at a table.

However, as I was leaving, I noticed that one of my old friends was sitting at a table and Mr. Bennett was taking their order. My friend had noticed me as well and signaled for me to stop by. I didn't want to interrupt Mr. Bennett while he was taking the order, so I placed my hand on his shoulder to let him know that I was there. Mr. Bennett turned around swiftly and smacked me on the top of the head with the stack of menus in his hand. My first instinct was to punch him, but I composed myself. As I was contemplating swinging on Mr. Bennett, my friend yelled in mixed laughter, "YO, what was that for!"

Mr. Bennett yelled at me and said, "Why did you punch me in the back like that?" My friend was bent over in laughter at this situation. I found myself not only angry but once again nervous and confused. I was not scared at all, but why was I nervous?

I didn't want to make any more of a scene. The other patrons in the dining room were already looking at us. I saw some customers shaking their heads in disgust. I simply walked away. I went and found Kassaundra. She and Travis were in the office talking. I burst into the office so quickly and with anger that they both looked at me with concern. I told them that Mr. Bennett had smacked me on top of the head with a stack of menus.

I thought that, at least this time, Kassaundra was going to take my concern seriously. Unfortunately, I was wrong again. She and Travis started laughing about the issue and not taking me seriously. Through laughter, Kassaundra stated that she couldn't believe Mr. Bennett would do anything like this. I was furious and stated, "So, you think that I am lying? I should've just hit him then." I looked at Travis and I could tell he didn't believe what happened either.

Kassaundra looked at me and said, "Surely, you are exaggerating." I couldn't take it any longer. I grabbed my things and left. I really wanted to never come back again, but my strained finances meant I couldn't quit.

It wasn't until the next afternoon when I came in that Kassaundra started to believe that what I said was true. One of our guests had called our corporate office to complain about the service from the prior day. On the email, it stated that the food took entirely too long and that the service was slow. They stated they could've dealt with all of that until a fight almost broke out in the dining room. They stated that a larger older man hit the younger man over the head with a stack of menus for no reason at all. The guest stated they would never come back to this location again.

Kassaundra looked at me, realizing that I was telling the truth. I looked back at her and stated, "You need to have my back sometimes." She swore that she was going to write Mr. Bennett up for misconduct, but I knew she never would.

For some reason, the entire crew must've found out about the incident between me and Mr. Bennett. When I walked into the kitchen, I saw the two servers that I hated the most in the corner talking: the Bitch and Malorie. The Bitch was laughing and Malorie, as per usual, was standing with her arms folded, frowning at the Bitch. It looked as if they were about to get into an altercation. I had just got into work and didn't want to start my day like this. I immediately went to them and attempted to break up the potential confrontation. I interrupted and asked if everything was okay. Of course, Malorie stood there mean mugging me like she wanted to spit on me.

The Bitch stated, "No, everything is okay. I was just asking Malorie to go and get me a stack of menus. Who knows, I may need them today!" Everyone in the kitchen bursted in laughter. Malorie didn't laugh but still stood there looking angry as ever. I couldn't stand this entire crew, especially Malorie and the Bitch.

If You Can't Beat Them, Join Them

I was pulling my hair out at work. I was trying my best to be a professional, but no matter how much I tried, my job became harder. It was hard to work at a place that held low standards. Kassaundra was a first-time general manager at a tough location. I know that Chris thought she could handle it, but no one should work there as a first-time GM.

On top of that, besides Travis, Kassaundra didn't have much of a support staff. Travis knew everything there was to know about being a manager. Then you had Franklin. Franklin was also knowledgeable on every aspect of the Blue Crab, but he was too unprofessional! You couldn't trust that Franklin would do the right thing. And Momma was only there to get a check. She wasn't interested in learning anything new or leading the team. She was as disinterested as you would ever see a manager be. Lastly, you had me. And I was no help at all. Yes, I was promoted because I was an excellent server who showed leadership ability, but there was no way in hell that I should've been sent to this restaurant. I was too young and too immature to handle this crowd of guests and crew. Admittedly, I wasn't mature enough to handle many of the indiscretions that would come my way over the years.

Truthfully, Travis was the only manager that should've been working there. Kassaundra knew her stuff, but she should've been granted an opportunity to learn her new position in an easier area. Franklin didn't need to be there because he was too much in his element. He acted just like the crew and the crowd. Come to think about it, they probably had him at this location because he would be too rough for any other clientele or crew. I definitely didn't need to be there. I should've been allowed to cut my teeth at a location where I could've learned more. And Momma shouldn't have been employed there in the first place. She needed to be a goat herder, where she could've smoked cigarettes and not had to engage with anyone.

I figured out that to last at this location I would have to find a way to adapt. It was tough because I didn't swear, hardly drank liquor, and didn't do any drugs. Most of the crew were not professional at all and didn't relate to someone reasoning with them. You had to get down and dirty with them. The managers that yelled here garnered the most respect.

Franklin probably had the most respect of them all, because he didn't mind cursing you out at any time. Franklin had no filter! Most of the crew would just laugh at Momma because when times got tough, she would always curse to herself. Anytime a guest would ask to see her, you would hear Momma cursing. Travis had the respect of the crew because he had no problem getting in your face and yelling at you. Also, the crew knew that if Travis got tired of you, he was going to figure out a way to fire you! The crew respected Kassaundra because she was the general manager and ultimately all the decisions lay with her. Kassaundra, like Travis, didn't mind getting in your face and yelling as well. Kassaundra was a big girl and menacing when she got mad. She would oftentimes send someone home and yell at them. However, it never meant nothing because she would hardly write them up for performance issues. So, it never mattered that she sent someone home if there was no consequences for their actions. Exhibit A, B, C, and D: Maria, the Bitch, Tom, and Mr. Bennett.

I still didn't want to become like those managers. I believed that it didn't take yelling at the top of your voice, cursing, or acting unprofessional for you to lead people. Unfortunately, I was in the minority with that thinking. I found that I was getting looser with the crew. The looser that I became, the looser the standards of the Blue Crab became. I started becoming their peer instead of their manager. So, although I was acting professional in my behavior, my failure to uphold the standards made me equally unprofessional anyway.

On one Friday night, I would throw the little bit of professionalism that I had straight out the window. I was the closer for the night and Franklin had come in for the mid-shift. I had worked the kitchen and Franklin worked the front. We had a good night. The guests were happy and so was the crew. Even the food looked good and came out in a timely fashion. It was a great night until about 10:00 p.m. Franklin was about to get off work.

Now, Franklin's getting off work meant that he was about to go sit at our bar and have a couple of drinks. Once Franklin was done and on his first drink, I transitioned to the front of the house. We only had an hour left before closing, so I started making a few cuts since we were slowing down. I talked to Franklin for a few minutes as he was downing a couple of shots. Everything was going good and surprisingly Franklin said that he was about to go home. He said that he had to close tomorrow, and he wanted to get a fair amount of rest. I said my goodbyes to him and started making rounds through the dining room.

In a matter of about fifteen minutes, the dining room was a mess. I counted at least seven tables that had not been bussed, let alone pre-bussed. The busser was nowhere in sight. As I was on the way to get the servers and the bussers to take care of this dining room, a table stopped me. They stated that they had been sitting down for almost thirty minutes without a server. Now, I knew they were exaggerating because most guests do when they are hungry. They probably weren't sitting there for thirty minutes, but it was probably about half that time. I apologized and told them that I was going to get a server over to them right away. I also told them that I would give them a complimentary appetizer for the inconvenience. As I attempted to make my way to the kitchen, I was stopped two additional times with the same complaint. I couldn't believe that this perfect night was slipping away from me.

I finally made it to the kitchen and observed that servers were in there eating food that the cooks said were extra. Who the hell made this call? We didn't have any extra food that we just gave out to the crew. The kitchen guys had decided to start breaking down the kitchen side early and two of the cooks were missing. I first found the servers who had not been to their tables and told them to get there immediately. They complained that the guests should be ashamed for coming in this late. I barked at them to get out to the tables immediately. Next, I told the expo to stop breaking down the kitchen and dress the food. We had food just sitting there getting cold and no one was running it. Lastly, I asked the main cook where the other two cooks were. He stated that they went outside to take a smoke break before we closed. I immediately ran outside to go and get them. I ushered them back in with the quickness.

Most of the crew were complaining that they were ready to go home. I was still having a hard time getting people to be productive. I pleaded with them that we only had fifteen minutes left and we just needed to get through it. My pleas didn't work and most of them still complained. I was having a hard time getting the food ran out to tables and the dining room became messier by the second. I ended up doing most of the food running myself. I desperately did not want another guest complaint. Once I saw that the crew was perfectly okay with me doing all the work, I became outraged. I told everyone that once we closed, we were going to have a mandatory all-crew meeting. A few of the people said they weren't going to stay because they were cut already. I was beyond mad and shouted out, "If anyone leaves, they don't work here anymore." I couldn't wait until we locked the doors. I don't think that I had ever been so mad and embarrassed before.

The meeting didn't start until about fifteen minutes after closing. I wanted to make sure that every food item went out as well as all drinks. Now people were helping me out because they wanted to get this meeting over with and done. Once everything was out, I started going around and telling everyone to meet me in the kitchen. I wanted everyone in there. As soon as I went in the kitchen, Maria tried to make a smart remark. I stopped her immediately and told everyone this was a meeting, but I was the only one who was going to do the talking. The mean chick, Malorie, was looking like she wanted to say something smart mouthed to me as well. I looked at her, daring her to say something. Fortunately for her, she didn't say a word. I was so frustrated and angry that I could hardly catch my breath. I started yelling at them all.

"I am completely disgusted with this crew. We had a great night until the last thirty minutes and then everyone stopped working. I swear to you that this behavior will never happen on my shift again."

The more I spoke, the louder my voice became. I called out every position in the restaurant and told them that if they ever gave up on me again that I would fire them and would not wait on Kassaundra to save them. I was now yelling and cursing.

Of course, Maria didn't want to be outdone and made the comment, "So you want us to work harder and be professional, but you are in here cursing. I'm pretty sure that Kassaundra and our corporate office would not be happy about that!"

A few of her flock started shaking their head in agreement! I wanted to come across the room and choke her.

Instead and, to my surprise, I yelled out, "When I am here, we will work better and as a team. And I don't give a fuck who y'all call. Matter of fact, here's my cards." I had a stack of my restaurant business cards in my pocket. I took them out and threw them across the room. "Fuckin get my name right if you want to call corporate."

I started walking out of the kitchen and a few of the team members clapped. Once I walked out of the kitchen, every table that was left in the dining room was staring at the kitchen door as I exited. This is when I realized that I was too loud. Truthfully, I couldn't care less. This crew needed to hear that! Not one guest said anything to me. I think they were relieved that someone got on top of this crew like this.

As everyone started to clean up and go home, several people came up to me and said how proud they were of me.

Simone came up and gave me a hug and a kiss on the cheek. She whispered softly in my ear, "That was sexy how you put everyone in check."

That whisper turned me on, but I tried not to let her notice it. I was desperately attempting to not become gentleman number four in her love quest. I just walked away from her. Surprisingly, Maria came up to me and apologized for stirring the pot.

"Good job, Carter. People needed to hear that. You gained a lot of respect tonight." In her drunken state, she smiled and said, "You might turn out to be a real manager after all!"

I wanted to choke her and pee in her coffee mug!

Respect

After I completely went bonkers on the crew, the word got around! When I went in to work the next day, that was all everyone was talking about. I was disappointed in myself for losing my composure, but the crew seemed to respect me more because of it. Even my fellow managers were talking about it, with exception of Kassaundra and Momma. Momma barely spoke to me at all and Kassaundra just didn't comment on it. Surely, her friends—oops, her workers—told her everything.

Although I never heard Travis curse at anyone, he commented to me, "I heard you got a little upset last night." I said that I did but was not happy about losing my composure. Travis commented, "Hey, sometimes you will have to get loud with people. Everyone thought they could run over you. Now they know they can't. Good job!"

I said thanks. It meant a lot to me that I had garnered respect from Travis. Everyone respected Travis and his authority, including the other managers.

However, Franklin walked up to me in the middle of the kitchen, laughing, and loudly said, "I heard you had to put these mutherfuckas in check last night. Good for you!"

I repeated the same thing that I had said to Travis about how I was disappointed that I lost my composure.

Franklin said, "Fuck that, you can't have no composure round here. You got to let loose on them." He started doing some dancing again and singing, "*Get loose on 'em, get loose.*" I shook my head and walked away.

As the night continued, Franklin wouldn't stop talking and joking with me. I tried to stay away from him as much as I could, but he kept coming around me. It was as if he thought that we were new best friends. I lost my composure once, and now he thought we were alike. Even his girl, Maria, started talking to me. Maria acted as if we never had an issue in the past. I wanted to remind her that I still wasn't cool with her, but I let it go.

The night ended up being a smooth and relatively good night. However, once we were about an hour away from closing, people started with the jokes again. We had one tray of food in the kitchen that no one had walked to a table and Maria came in the kitchen and started to pretend to be me. She was laughing the entire time as she said, "Somebody better walk this food. We will work as a team! And if y'all are mad at me, call corporate. Here's my fuckin cards, get my name right!" As she said cards, she flung some of my cards in the air. Everyone in the kitchen broke out in laughter. I even thought that it was funny. I smiled and walked away.

At the end of the night, after we had cashed out the remainder of the servers and were waiting for the kitchen crew to finish cleaning up, Franklin asked me if I wanted to have a drink from the bar. I was a little reluctant. I didn't want to get fired for having a drink, although I had seen Kassaundra drinking a margarita on several occasions. I said, "Sure!" I went to the back to check on the kitchen guys. They still had a least an hour left before they would be ready. The last thing I wanted was for the crew to walk out and see me having a drink. I went back up to the front to have a drink and Franklin was already behind the bar making a mixed drink. To my surprise, however, Angie was also sitting at the bar. I tried to turn around, but Franklin waved me over.

He said, "Whatcha drinking?"

I told him that I just wanted to have a margarita. My thought was that I was going to have what I saw Kassaundra drinking on several occasions. After all, if I got into trouble, then at least I was drinking the same thing Kassaundra was drinking. Now Franklin and Angie were drinking Hennesy straight. Angie was already on what looked to be her third drink.

Halfway through my first margarita, someone knocked on the front window. I almost pooped on myself. A million thoughts were going through my head. What if it was Kassaundra? Or worse, what if it was my area director? I also didn't want it to be one of our crewmembers. Franklin went to the front door and let whoever it was come in. I thought to myself that my short career as a manager was about to be over.

As I braced myself for what was about to happen next, I heard a lot of laughing. I instantly knew whose loud voice this was. It was Maria. As soon as she saw me, she started laughing even louder! She still had on her work uniform, although her shirt was completely unbuttoned, showing her pink bra and her perky boobs.

Maria looked at both Franklin and Angie and said, "How did y'all get him to have a drink?" She next looked at me and said, "I didn't know that you even knew how to relax!"

I grabbed my margarita and started drinking it before I said something ignorant. I still wasn't a fan of hers. Maria just went right behind the bar and started making herself a drink. I could tell this wasn't her first time going behind this bar and making her own drink. She had a sense of familiarity with it. She poured herself a tall Absolut and cranberry. I had never seen so much liquor in one drink. She had put maybe three small cubes of ice in her glass. The rest was mainly Absolut with a splash of cranberry. She came from behind the bar and sat right next to me. Franklin looked at us sitting next to each other and said, "Awww, look at you two sitting next to each other. Y'all made up!"

Once again, I just took a sip of my margarita to stop from saying anything. I still don't know why Maria decided to sit next to me. This bitch was acting like we didn't just have an altercation a few weeks before. Maria must've been reading my mind because she stated to Franklin and Angie, "His little mean ass still hasn't spoken to me. And you know me, I don't usually give a fuck, but I respected the way he let everyone have it the other day."

I couldn't take it anymore. I said, "You respected the way I handled it as long as it doesn't pertain to you, right?"

She bursted out in a drunken laugh and said, "Yeah, papi, just don't come for me. I run this shit."

I was about to lose my cool and Franklin stepped in and said, "Carter, she's just kidding." I was still fuming, and Maria looked as if she wanted the fight to start. I was ready for her drunken ass.

Luckily, Angie was there. She was looking at the television the entire time, but she finally looked at Maria and told her, "Maria, sit your drunk ass down and shut up! That man ain't trying to do nothing but his job. Leave him alone!"

I looked at Maria and said, "Yeah, you should listen to Angie. Sit your drunk ass down and shut up!"

As I was preparing for the fight, Maria seductively caressed her breast and said, "Oh shit, I think I am in love with your little mean ass. You mean and got some balls! You better be lucky that you are too short for me!" At this, they all burst into laughter. I even smiled a little bit at this as well.

As I was finishing my margarita, Maria was already done with her vodka and cranberry and on her way back to the bar to make another drink. She ended up not only making a drink for herself, but for Angie and Franklin as well. I was still astonished that she was so fluent behind the bar. I didn't want another drink, but she ended up making me a drink as well.

I asked her what this drink was called. She told me it was called Boys to Men. She laughingly said, "It will put some hair on your chest and may even get you to grow taller." She thought this was so funny and was bent over in laughter.

Franklin said to her, "You are one mean bitch!" I paid her no attention. I was trying my best to drink this unbelievably strong drink. This drink was so strong that it burned going down. I started to feel like hair was not only growing on my chest, but it was growing on my feet as well.

We continued to talk, and they continued to drink. I was done and could barely drink what Maria had poured for me. I asked them how often they did this. Franklin said that he drank every night that he worked unless Kassaundra was working. Franklin stated that Kassaundra didn't mind if he had one beer or a glass of wine, but that was about it. I asked if he drank when Travis was here. Franklin said, "I don't give a fuck if Travis is here, he ain't my boss!"

Maria playfully said, "Don't talk about my man like that!"

I said, "Your man?"

She said, "That's right! His tall ass can get this whenever he's ready!" As she was talking and fantasizing about Travis, she once again started to caress her own breast. I shook my head, but I started to get it. Maria wouldn't listen to no one except for Travis. Even if Kassaundra or her best friend Franklin told her what to do, she would have some smart comment, but she would never say anything to Travis. I recalled once that Travis had barked at Maria to quiet down in the kitchen. Maria smiled and said, "No problem, Big Daddy!"

I stayed a little longer to get sober but I wanted to go home. I was high off that drink Maria had made for me. I couldn't imagine trying to drive home like this. Most importantly, I couldn't imagine how they were going to drive home. If I was almost drunk, they had to already be over the limit.

Just as I was about to leave, the two dishwashers walked up to the front to say that they were done. I was embarrassed that they saw me having a drink, but that embarrassment quickly went away. The next thing you knew, they were sitting down at the bar. Franklin went behind the bar and poured a couple of beers for them. I could tell they were used to this as well. I got up and left.

Training

Now that I had been here for a while, I was getting used to the crew and the guests. I learned how to not get run over. Although each manager had their different style, I was learning what style worked best for me.

Kassaundra used intimidation. She was a big girl, and she had a menacing personality. There was something about her that I couldn't put my finger on, but she seemed as if she knew people that could make you disappear. She always looked angry and ready for an argument.

Travis was to the point and serious. He played no games with anyone (guest or crew) and everyone knew this. He rarely cracked a smile and was thorough with everything he did. He was viewed as intimidating because he was so serious.

Momma didn't want any confrontation at all. She would just give you what you wanted to stop you from even talking to her.

Franklin was GHG—gay, hood, and ghetto, so he used this to his advantage. This restaurant was a challenging restaurant and both crew and guests were hood. He would curse and fuss at the guests, but somehow this worked for him. I think Kassaundra hated his guts, however. I could tell Franklin hated Kassaundra just as much.

My style was to try to be as professional as I could and to try to have fun. After many trials and errors, I adapted the style of putting myself in the shoes of the customers. I would imagine how I would feel if it were me.

Looking at everything from a customer's viewpoint helped me out a lot. The first thing that I realized was, except for a few servers, most of the servers weren't that good. We didn't really have any rude servers, but they knew nothing about the menu. It was quite embarrassing. I started quizzing my servers during their check-ins to test their menu knowledge. Most of them didn't know descriptions, portion sizes, or flavor profile.

From my previous stops as a server and a certified trainer for the Blue Crab, I was excellent at training. I was surprised at the low level of knowledge, seeing that Travis was the service manager. I think his focus was on numbers and trying to get promoted, that he lost track of the essentials that made restaurants great. Service is the most important thing, next to food taste and quality. I was able to convince both Travis and Kassaundra to allow me to re-train the entire staff. I also said that I wanted to take over training for all new hires that came in.

Most of the servers were defiant about me doing their training, but I didn't care. I thought it was going to be Maria and the Bitch complaining the most, but it was Malorie who came to me upset about the training. I told her that although she was a good server, I wanted to move them from *good* to *great*. Also, due to the lack of teamwork, we were getting an absurd amount of complaints. After I explained this to her, she just looked at me and walked away. I couldn't stand her.

Once the meetings began, I explained to the servers that I was sick of getting guest complaints about simple things they should've known. I took the next three days and completely re-trained them on every step of serving. We went over body language, order taking, pivot points, table greeting, pre-bussing, bussing, liquor knowledge, and food knowledge. I taught them how to do a menu tour as well as suggestive selling. We even went over wine demonstration and the proper technique to open a wine bottle. I taught them the importance of not just being an order taker but someone that always gave five-star service. We would role play doing the table greets and ordering. At the end of the training class, many servers told me that it was informative and they learned things they hadn't known before. I was pleased with everyone for giving me their attention and for their learning, except for Maria and the Bitch. Neither of them attended the meetings. For whatever reason, they were excused from the meetings. Some of the other servers were mad they were excused, but I was happy. I didn't want the dramatics.

Besides the two favorites not attending the meetings, I only had one other person that would not make it through this training process. On the first day of the training meetings, I had given everyone one item off the menu they would have to be able to describe in terms of the taste, the texture, and the preparation by their next shift. Everyone, except for this one particular guy Emmanuelle, was able to do this successfully. Some of them even asked for me to give them another item to describe. This guy was the only one that would not even attempt to give a description.

I had a problem with Emmanuelle the first week that I worked here. From my time as a server, I remembered when we had a stinky server and the managers wouldn't address it. I thought it was pitiful on their part to not address it. So, when I came across one of my servers that also had a foul odor, I decided to address it immediately. I tried to handle it delicately, but he acted as if he was offended for me bringing up his hygiene. I should have acted like Franklin and said, "You need to go somewhere and soak your nuts in the bathtub." However, I didn't say that, but I did advise him that customers and fellow coworkers commented on his smell. He didn't want to believe me and said that no one had ever said anything before. I apologized that it wasn't stated to him previously, but the fact was that he had a smell and must take care of it. He commented that this is how he smelled and that he wasn't going to change anything. I ended up taking him off the schedule until he decided to take care of it. He continued to come in over the next three shifts until he realized that he just wasted his gas money. I would not let him work until he took care of his smell. On the fourth day, I guess he decided to take a bath because he finally didn't have a stench.

That was my second week working with him that he tried to give me a hard time. Now, a few months later, he wanted to challenge me again. Just like I did with every other server, I asked him to give me his description of a food item.

"Emmanuelle, what are the ingredients of our Signature Blue Crab Cakes? Also, what is it garnished with and what sauce is it served with?" I asked.

"I know it has crab in it, but that's about it. Not sure what else is in them. I haven't had time to study the menu!" he replied.

I told him that he should take a menu home and study it.

"Look, Carter, I am in school with a full course load. When I study, it surely will not be anything from the Blue Crab," was his reply.

Although I was pissed, I told him that he could work today,

but if he didn't know it tomorrow that he couldn't be a server for the Blue Crab.

"Okay, I will try to learn it, but I'm not going to make any promises!"

I replied, "No problem! I will try to keep you employed, but I'm not going to make any promises."

He shrugged and walked away. The next shift, he came in and had the audacity to not know the menu item. I asked him if he looked at the menu.

He told me, "Naw, man, I didn't have time for that."

I was shocked with his honesty. I advised him that effective immediately he could not be a server for the Blue Crab, but I could offer him a position as a bus boy or a dishwasher. He was beside himself with anger.

"You can't do that. When will Kassaundra be in to work?"

I advised him that Kassaundra was already in. He went back to the kitchen to talk to her. A few minutes later, Kassaundra asked me to come to the office to talk. When I got in, Emmanuelle was already in there. I looked at Kassaundra with disgust. If she thought about going against me on this one, I was going to go off.

Surprisingly, she was calm. She asked Stinky Boy if he studied what I had given him.

He explained to Kassaundra, "I already told Carter that I don't have time to be studying the menu." To my surprise, Kassaundra looked at me and then at Stinky Boy.

She said, "Well, I am going to support Carter's decision. If you can't take the time to learn basic menu items, then I don't want to take the time to have you as a server with us."

I wasn't sure what was more surprising: that she had taken my side, or that Stinky Boy was crying. Not only was he crying, but he was boo-hooing. He practically started begging for his job. Why didn't he show this same passion about studying the menu or simply taking a bath? It didn't make me feel bad at all. All I could think about was getting out of this office. Don't cry now, Stinky Boy! I bet that even his tears were stinky!

I was pleasantly surprised that Kassaundra had my back for the first time. Although, I knew it wasn't about having my back. When Stinky Boy attempted to disrespect her, she was done with him.

Train the Trainer

Although Kassaundra had finally upheld one of my decisions, we still weren't on that good of terms. I heard that she was a little upset that I was quizzing the crew daily on menu items. She had her favorites and they walked around liked they owned the building. Primarily, they would work lunch shifts when she would work. This way they were under her protection.

I didn't care if they were her favorites. Either you were good, or you weren't. I wasn't going to tiptoe around them because they were Kassaundra's favorites. Now, some of the favorites were getting quizzed on menu items and they didn't like it. I walked in one day and overheard a couple of her favorites talking. Of course, the Bitch was the ringleader. She stated that Kassaundra was pissed that I kept quizzing them on things and that I didn't even know all my stuff. I didn't let it bother me or think it was true. Why would she be upset about me quizzing my servers?

One shift, the Bitch was working and I had quizzed her on some menu items. Out of nowhere, Kassaundra came storming around the corner. In the middle of the kitchen, she confronted me very aggressively. Once again, I was nervous and shaking. She asked me to stop quizzing people every day and said that I was embarrassing her.

"I am just trying to strengthen the crew on menu knowledge. This is what I am supposed to do, correct?"

"Well you could still use some training yourself. Do you think that you know everything about management?" Kassaundra questioned.

Before I could reply, she berated me with questions that I had no answer to.

She asked me, "What was our ROS for last month?"

I told her that I have never heard of ROS before.

She said, "That is the Return on Sales!"

Next, she asked, "What was our EBITDA for last month?"

I once again didn't know the answer to that.

She said, "EBITDA stands for Earnings before Interest, Taxes, Depreciation, and Amortization." She was trying to embarrass me but didn't realize that she was making my point. Some of the servers were laughing in the background.

She said, "How does it feel to get questioned on things that you don't know?"

I replied, "Kassaundra, I never heard of these terms before, but as my boss you should be going over those terminologies with me, just as I am going over things with my crew. Thank you for sharing the knowledge."

This made her angrier. She told me that I needed to stop embarrassing the crew. I wanted to say that the crew isn't the problem, it was her favorites that she didn't want me to mess with. But I didn't dare say this to my boss.

Over the next couple of weeks, Kassaundra barely spoke to me unless she wanted to complain about an order I messed up on. Mind you, orders that I was never trained on. Instead of getting upset, she could've sat down with me and gone over the details.

Finally, after I had been continuously messing up the orders, Franklin and Travis pulled me to the side and said they were going to help me out.

Travis started helping me out on how to submit invoices. I'm not sure if I was having a hard time retaining what he was teaching me or if he was a bad instructor. He would go over something quickly and never really show me how to do it. He was just doing it himself. He would get impatient if he had to show me something more than once. He didn't understand that I wasn't getting it the first time.

One thing that I remembered from training was that everyone learns differently and that one size doesn't fit all. Travis didn't believe in that methodology. After working with him a few times on invoices, I told him that I felt like I perfected it. He seemed proud of himself for being a great instructor. Truth be told, I still didn't understand it fully, but I didn't want to work with him on this any longer. Although he knew his stuff, his ability to teach it was awful.

Surprisingly, Franklin was a much better teacher than Travis. I was in the office trying to figure out an invoice for fish and Franklin asked me what I was doing and why was it taking me so long. I told him that I was doing a fish invoice. After he saw how I was doing it and how many steps I was taking, he said, "Travis must've shown you how to do this. I don't know what the fuck he be doing, but let me show you."

I was reluctant to learn from him, but I decided to listen anyway. He had a simplistic way of showing me how to do something that just made sense. After doing invoices with him once, I truly did understand it. Travis was showing me too many steps to do something, whereas Franklin kept it simple. I thanked him for showing me this and said I understood it much better now.

He next taught me how to do a produce order. He had me print up the ordering form for produce and had me go in and take the inventory for it. This was a piece of cake because I had done produce orders many times. There were about twenty items on our produce sheet, and I had this down to a science. I had counted and put everything on my inventory sheet in about five minutes. I came back to the office and handed the sheet to Franklin. Proudly, I told him that I was done.

He looked at me and said, "Bullshit? Follow me to the cooler."

He was doubting my skills, but I followed him anyway. I had the clipboard with my produce inventory on it. I wanted to show him that I was indeed finished.

Before we walked in the cooler he said, "Carter, leave the clipboard on the counter. You won't need that yet."

I looked confused. "Why would we not bring in the clipboard into the cooler if we are about to count everything on the clipboard?"

He explained, "It's impossible to do an order without first organizing the cooler. When doing an order, you should be accomplishing three things: organization, rotation, and sanitizing. Now go get the step ladder and a sanitizer bucket and towel."

I came back with both and he told me to watch him. He got up on the step ladder and got to it. I was watching as he started shifting boxes and rotating product. There were boxes on the top rack that I had counted. However, I hadn't noticed that there were boxes behind them hidden. He made sure that we pulled everything out, looked at the label and the date. He also cut the box tops off and opened boxes. I had counted these as whole boxes because someone had folded the boxes back in, but I hadn't looked inside them. Some of these boxes had only one item in them.

Franklin told me that when doing a count, it was important to touch each and every box. As he was touching boxes and looking in them, he was also organizing the boxes and ensuring all labels were facing out. All like items were placed together. He was also wiping down and sanitizing as he was counting. When he was complete, the cooler looked great.

"Now you can go and get the clipboard," he instructed.

We recounted together and I noticed that my first count was completely off. If Franklin hadn't recounted, we would've been out of several items the next day. I was appreciative that he took the time to show me how to do the order the correct way. I wondered why Kassaundra couldn't have done this with me. I was impressed at how thorough Franklin was despite him being so unprofessional.

When we finished putting the order in, he told me, "Now don't fuck up these orders anymore!" When I first started managing here, I would've been offended. However, I accepted this was just how he is.

The more Franklin and I worked together, the more I had an appreciation for his work method. I mostly closed with him on the weekends, so we would always drink at closing. And yes, Angie and Maria would be there as well. I didn't even care if the dishwashers saw me drinking any longer either. I would learn more about the business after closing from talking with Franklin than I would learn during the open hours working with Kassaundra. I would also learn all the gossip after hours as well. Franklin and Maria knew all of it. I found out they would hold many parties at their houses, and most of the crew would end up at those.

Note to self: Never, never, never, go to one of these parties.

Bonding (or Not)

As the months passed, I started creating more of a rapport with Franklin and Travis. Unfortunately, the more I talked to them, the more I found myself creating more distance between me and Kassaundra. I felt that Kassaundra disliked Franklin and wanted him out of her restaurant. Although she was rough around the edges and a borderline gangster, Franklin was just too much. He was loud and flamboyant. The time he came to work with pink hair was just too much for Kassaundra. He had on some too-tight khaki pants with a Gucci belt and shoes, with a pink shirt and pink socks to go with his pink hair. Kassaundra almost lost it. She didn't try to compose herself.

She stopped Franklin in his tracks and said, "You must be here to eat as a guest, because you are not about to work as a manager in my restaurant looking like that!"

Franklin said, "Looking like what?"

Kassaundra said, "Looking ghetto as hell!"

Franklin was ready for the argument. He said, "My entire assembly is within company spec. And how you going to call me ghetto?"

Kassaundra barked, "I didn't call you ghetto, I stated that you are looking ghetto. You can't work as a manager or a team member with pink hair and you know this, Franklin."

Kassaundra just stood there, waiting for Franklin's next move. By this time, other team members started to gather around to see what was about to go down. Kassaundra, not ever wanting to lose, said, "Franklin, you need to go home and decide if you want to work here or not. You will not be a manager for me and have pink hair."

Franklin was slick, but he knew that he wasn't going to win this stalemate with Kassaundra. Not wanting to be outdone though, he said, "I am not about to go home, honey."

Kassaundra looked like she was about to come strangle him. Angie happened to see the commotion and told Franklin, "Dude, just go home."

Franklin said, "Girl, y'all trippin" and flung off his wig. "It's just a wig!" He looked at Kassaundra and said, "Can I work now?"

Kassaundra just looked at him and walked away. Everyone started laughing and Franklin started dancing again. What a crazy place this was!

As far as Travis went, I think Kassaundra wanted him out of the building as well. Travis tried to act as if he was the general manager and he garnered the respect of one, although this was Kassaundra's restaurant. Kassaundra didn't realize it, or maybe she did, but she managed by intimidation. She would yell at the crew and make them cry, but if they came with a sob story and apologized, she would let them continue working. As long as you didn't come after her, you were okay. Most people wouldn't have thought about coming after her because she was too gangster.

Travis knew the rule that every termination must flow through the general manager, but he didn't care. He knew that despite team members getting sent home, Kassaundra would allow them to come back. Travis made sure that he completed a paper trail and would always let our director, Chris, know what happened before he updated Kassaundra. I think she disliked him for that.

I never really developed a relationship with Momma either. She couldn't care less about anything in the restaurant. She did nothing but swipe her card whenever a team member needed something. She didn't ask any questions about why you needed something done or removed from a check; it just didn't bother her. She was never proactive and always steered to the way of the team members.

One evening, it was me and Momma working, and she barely spoke to me the entire evening. It didn't bother me at all because she never had anything to talk about. She was always cursing and complaining about either the crew or the guests. Never did she have anything meaningful to say or had she ever shown me anything new. She got along with Franklin because they both smoked, swore, and cursed a lot, but I rarely saw her speak to Travis. Travis wasn't so tolerant of Momma and her ineffectiveness.

Anyhow, this night was a busy night and we had quite a few guest complaints. Instead of Momma attempting to correct the issues, she sided with the crew. I heard her complaining and saying things like, "These motherfuckas should've just stayed home" or "I am not buying shit for these assholes."

Momma irritated me so bad. She was getting guest complaints because she wasn't aware of what was going on in the dining room. Instead, she was always outside smoking or sitting down at a booth in the anchor doing crossword puzzles.

Since the restaurant was having so many problems, we had started having security every night. Momma would lean on security to handle problems. If a customer was upset and got a little loud, Momma would never handle it. She would just send security. The customers would become more upset when security came around and would demand a manager come by. The guests didn't want security—they just wanted the problem fixed. Momma was creating more work for herself.

She got so frustrated this night that she decided she was going to close the restaurant fifteen minutes early. Now, we could be terminated for making this decision without permission from our area director. I tried to act as if I didn't know that she had closed early; however, five minutes to our actual closing time we had some customers leaving. As they were exiting the building, some other customers were approaching the door at the same time. These customers had no idea we were closed because technically we weren't. Momma had already instructed the hostess to tell anyone approaching the door that we were closed. Now, any other time the crew didn't want to follow orders, but when it is the wrong thing to do, they had no problem following orders.

Unfortunately, I happened to be walking past the lobby when the guests approached the hostess. As they approached, the hostess immediately stated that we were closed. The customers looked at their watches and said, "We still have five minutes, don't we?"

They looked at me and I said, "Yes, we are still open."

I wanted no part of Momma's wrongdoings. I wished I hadn't been in the lobby. The hostess looked at me as if I were the devil. Another couple came in right behind them and I made sure they were also sat. When Momma found out that I had sat the two tables, she became outraged. She went to the kitchen and had a fit. She was so upset that I thought she was going to have a heart attack. Her complexion turned fire red and her veins were popping out everywhere. She was so unnecessarily angry that I made the mistake of laughing.

When I laughed, she turned around and started toward me while cursing under her breath. I tried to calm her down and was still laughing, but I began shaking once again. I was so upset that I was shaking because truly I was not afraid of this old lady or anyone else. Why was I shaking like this? Momma would eventually calm herself down, but I don't think we ever conversed after that incident. Momma ended up quitting a few weeks after that and I was elated. She wasn't a true manager anyway.

FRANKLIN

After Momma left, I ended up working more shifts with Franklin. The more I worked with him, the less he bothered me. I still thought he was unprofessional but felt bad for judging him; he was just very outspoken. He would speak what was on his mind and never sugarcoat it. Some guests loved him for being outspoken but other guests disliked him much the same.

The guests that loved him would often give him compliments. He would tell them to call our 1-888 number to corporate or to mention his name on our surveys. He would do this to prove a point to Kassaundra and our area director, Chris.

Kassaundra always complained about Franklin's vulgarity with the customers to Chris. She wanted him out of her restaurant. However, Kassaundra couldn't justify it because he had so many compliments. Franklin had all his friends calling the corporate office and singing his praises. Franklin had friends that came to the restaurant almost every day. I couldn't understand how people could come out to eat so often. Usually, Franklin would have Maria wait on them. They seemed to all know Maria as well. These guests never complained about service or food even if it took too long. For the most part, these guests were always happy and well fed. I never really paid attention to their bill before, but most of these guests ordered several drinks, an appetizer, and entrées. Once again, I wondered what these people did for a living to be able to afford meals like this every day, let alone every week.

In contrast and to Kassaundra's point, the guests that disliked Franklin were probably just as many. As mentioned earlier, Franklin had no filter when it came to what he said and how he acted. There would be times that guests complained about things and Franklin would barely do anything for them. Instead of acting like a manager or a professional, he would make abusive comments. Now, Franklin said what every manager thought but would never say. Franklin would just say it.

For example, if a guest came in ten minutes to close and we were out of something, he would tell them, "We are about to close in ten minutes. You know that you don't come into a restaurant when they are about to close."

On other occasions when we would be busy on a Saturday night and guests would complain about how long they were waiting to be seated, Franklin would tell them, "It's Saturday night and you knew it was going to be a long wait!" Guests would often be appalled by his answers and so was I! The crew would laugh at him on some things he would say. Although it was funny, he should not have been talking in this manner as a manager.

There were times where a guest complained that they found hair in their food. Some of the guests would be so upset that they didn't want anything else to eat and demanded that the food be taken off the check. This would upset Franklin. I heard him respond in the kitchen, in front of the crew, "Now this bitch acting brand new about some damn hair. These bitches in here be acting like they never gave head before and got some hair caught in their throat." I was amazed at the things he would say, but the crew would agree and laugh along with him.

Once, we (the managers) were sitting in the dining room having lunch and the guests seated in the booth next to us were three elderly ladies. One of the elderly ladies at the table had a large magnifying glass that she was using to look over the menu. Franklin saw this and busted out in laughter. He said, "Oh shit, look at that Big Ass Magnifying Glass!" I instantly put my head down in embarrassment. Fortunately for us, the ladies' hearing was on the same level as their sight, because they didn't hear a thing!

On a couple of occasions, Franklin bit off more than he could chew! He ended up talking to the wrong guy in this manner. This customer had been sitting at the bar. The bartender was swamped and couldn't keep up with both the amount of drinks that were being rang up and his customers. Instead of the bartender asking for help, he just ignored the guests. This one gentleman had been sitting at the bar for at least fifteen minutes with the bartender continuously walking past him. The customer couldn't take it any longer. He got up from the bar and went to the host podium, where he asked for a manager. It was probably another fifteen minutes before Franklin managed to come up to the bar to see him. Once he came behind the bar, he was nonchalant as he approached the customer. The customer was set back by his disposition right away. Franklin never introduced himself and just came directly to him and asked if he needed help with anything.

The customer asked Franklin who he was, since he didn't introduce himself.

Franklin rudely responded, "You asked for a manager, didn't you? Well, I am the manager!" The customer was shocked on how he responded and stated that he couldn't believe how unprofessional he was. I guess Franklin had enough, so he just walked away from the customer while he was still talking.

The customer stood up from his bar stool and spoke loudly, stating, "I wasn't done speaking to you!"

Franklin responded, "Oh yeah, you are done!"

The customer had lost his cool with him. Luckily, I was walking around the corner at the time this guy was approaching Franklin. He had already stepped behind the bar and was cursing at him and pointing his finger in his face. Franklin didn't back down, but he wasn't running his mouth either. It was in this moment that he realized he'd spoken badly to the wrong person. I came behind the bar quickly and told the guy to leave. He continued to yell at Franklin, so I had to raise my voice even louder. He quickly turned from Franklin to me.

He yelled at me, saying, "Who the fuck is this loud, gay bitch that is here working as a so-called manager? He picked the wrong one today!"

I again told him that he had to leave, equaling his raised octave. As the guy was talking to me, Franklin started walking from behind the bar. The guest saw this and said, "Yeah, bitch, walk away. Talk to me like that again and I will fuck you up!"

I said louder, "Sir, you must leave now!"

He turned and looked at me and said, "You can get fucked up too!"

He was so angry that I was sure that we were about to get into a fight. I stood there getting ready for what was about to go down, but he just walked past me, gathered his things, and left. I was glad that nothing happened, but I was once again upset because I was shaking nervously. I just didn't get it. Why was I shaking all the time when placed in a confrontation? The more that this occurred, the more I was concerned. This had never happened before I started working here!

* * *

There was another time in which I had to step in and save Franklin from a volatile situation. We had a dishwasher that worked for us who was an ex-boxer and ex-con. This guy was in his early fifties but was still in awesome shape. You could tell that he still worked out and could probably take out most guys half his age in a fist fight. He used to always give us pointers on working out, as well as fight techniques. For the most part, he was a pleasurable guy. He liked to talk a lot and would take too long to finish up his job because he would practically have a conversation with anyone who talked to him.

Franklin couldn't stand him and would often give him a hard time about his productivity. Franklin was in his rights to coach someone on performance, but he didn't coach. He just cursed and fussed at people. You can do this with some folks, but this doesn't work on everyone.

Franklin continued to badger the dish guy constantly. He was not being productive at first, but once Franklin said something to him about his productivity, he picked up the pace. The problem was, Franklin would never stop once he got going. Every time that he would pass him, he would make a comment. I heard Franklin say to him, "Hurry your slow ass up!"

He looked at him and said, "Mr. Franklin, sir, please don't talk to me like that!" It was like Franklin was a shark and saw blood in the water. This was typically how he was. He would pick on people until they folded or started to cry.

I went and talked to the dishwasher and told him that I would get Franklin to leave him alone and I could tell he was upset. He thanked me for speaking with him and said that he really needed this job.

I talked to Franklin once and told him to leave the guy alone, but he wouldn't stop. Probably about an hour later, someone told me the telephone was for me. I picked up the line and it was our dishwasher. He asked me to come outside and said he would be on the side of the building. I asked him what he was doing outside! He said that he couldn't look at Franklin anymore and could I please come outside.

I went outside and I could tell this dude was heated. His eyes were bloodshot red, and you could see every muscle flexing through his shirt.

I asked him, "Sir, are you okay?"

"No, Mr. Carter, I am not okay. I can't come back in there. I quit."

I asked why he decided to quit.

"Mr. Carter, that Franklin has been talking so bad to me that I had to hurry up and get out of this building. Could you please bring me my check and I will kindly leave?"

I told him that I could absolutely get his check, but I didn't want him to quit. I also told him that he could come inside and get his check.

He said, "Mr. Carter, I am afraid to come into that building and see that so-called manager ever again. I don't know what I would do to him. I left because if he said anything else to me, I swear I would've knocked his head off. I've been to the penitentiary before and it won't be no thang for me to go back. Please go and get my check, sir!"

I went in and got his check and brought it back out to him.

"Thank you, Carter, for being professional and treating people with respect. I'm going to tell you this: had Franklin been a straight man, I would've broken his neck."

I believed him. When I went back inside, Franklin asked where the dish guy went. I told him that he just quit and that I gave him his final check.

He commented, "What a pussy. He walked out when I wasn't around. He better be glad that I didn't see him trying to walk out. I would've let his punk ass have it."

Franklin had no idea how close he was to getting severely beat up. This guy was really upset and would've hurt him extremely bad. Franklin needed to learn how to talk to people. I hoped someone didn't hurt him one day!

No-Nonsense Travis

Now Travis was completely different than Franklin. He would only go off on you if you tried him. You really had to push his buttons. He focused on being professional, but once he lost it, there was no turning back. There were a few occasions in which Travis had to deal with extremely difficult guests. He would tell them they had to leave immediately. He would also do this with the crew. Travis played no games! I was happy that we had security because on a few occasions, the situation would become uncontrollable. Not that Travis couldn't handle it, but having security helped de-escalate customer involvement. I didn't understand how Travis could let people take him over the edge. I had this feeling that Travis couldn't have cared less about losing his job. No one was going to disrespect him.

On one occasion, we had a guest that was using profanity loudly in the dining room. Travis went to him and politely asked him to lower his voice. The guest looked at Travis, ignored him, and continued cursing in a loud manner. Travis once again asked the gentleman to calm down.

The guy looked at Travis and said, "This is a free country and I can talk any way that I want to."

I saw Travis trying to keep his composure as he tried to

explain that we had other customers within earshot eating—some with children—and that his language wasn't appropriate.

The guest said loudly, "I don't give a fuck about some other guests or their children."

That was it. Travis wasn't trying to play nice anymore. Travis told the guy that he must leave the building immediately.

The customer said, "Or what?"

I could tell that Travis wanted to put his hands on the guy and the customer saw this as well. The customer stood up to face Travis. Travis and the customer were looking at each other eye to eye. Travis was a tall guy and so was this guy. It looked like it was going to turn ugly because we all knew that Travis wasn't going to back down and it looked as if this customer wasn't going to give in either. It was about to go down!

Fortunately, someone had informed our security what was going on and our security officer stepped in and defused the situation. Now, don't get me wrong, Travis was about to handle his business, but the security officer handled it gracefully. Our security officer, Mims, came in and immediately stepped in between them. He wasn't as tall as either Travis or the customer, but he wasn't no small man either. Mims had a smooth but demanding presence. Mims turned to Travis and told Travis that he had it. Travis didn't want to back down so Mims looked at him, put his hand on Travis's shoulder, and told him to walk away.

Mims was probably the only person I knew that could've gotten Travis to settle down and walk away. They were good friends and Travis respected him a lot. If it had been anyone else, it would've been a problem. Travis eventually walked away. As Travis walked away, the customer made smart comments toward him. Travis stopped in his steps, but Mims said, "Don't do it, man! I got it!"

Once Travis was far enough away, I saw Mims talking to the guy. The guy tried to get loud, but Mims was able to get him to calm down. I don't know what Mims said to him, but he started walking toward the door with the guest. The next thing we knew, the guest shook Mims's hand and left the premises. I don't know what would've happened if Mims wasn't in the building.

As Travis and I started working more and more together, I would usually focus on the dining room and he would focus on the kitchen. I wanted to deal with the hostile guest situations rather than have Travis do it. I didn't want our restaurant to get shot up one day because Travis beat someone up. Our closes together would be much different than my closes with Franklin. He would let the crew stay and drink, but he would keep the bartender on, and the crew would pay for their drinks. Most of the crew wouldn't hang around too long, because they preferred when Franklin closed because everyone drank for free then. Travis would never have a drink and when it was time to go, we weren't hanging around while everyone else drank. He made everyone get out.

Travis did drink but he wanted no part of drinking at the restaurant with the crew. He asked me to go have a drink at another bar on a few occasions. We would go and kick back a couple of drinks. I found out that Travis was a pretty cool guy. He was more laid back out of the restaurant. I found out that he had a couple of businesses that he was involved in with his friends. When he wasn't at work, he was usually out of town conducting business. He often told me that it was important to have more than one stream of income. He told me that he really wanted to get promoted to a general manager, but he still wasn't going to put all his eggs in one basket. He also added that he didn't know if he was going to have to choke somebody one day.

I found out that he was an ex–FBI agent, but he didn't share with me why he wasn't still with them. He did share with me stories on FBI takedowns that he was part of. He was used to using a lot of authority. In his past, when he spoke people jumped. He shared that he had a problem when people didn't show him respect. The FBI was very structured and if your superior asked you to do something, it was not a suggestion. Travis stated that his background made him both good and terrible as a restaurant manager. He stated that the structure, the control, and the authority put him in great shape to be successful as a manager, but also dealing with people who had no structure was a challenge for him. He admitted that he was a control freak and had anger issues. He also admitted that having Mims there really helped him out. He stated that he would've probably lost his job already had it not been for Mims. I agreed with that assessment.

Over time, Travis and I would hang out more outside of work. He was cool. We started going to the gym together. I found out that Travis was a ladies' man. He always had a woman calling him. He was juggling about four different women. He said that he was single and didn't mind going out but was looking for something serious.

I asked him what was up with him and Maria.

He looked at me and said, "Naw, that chick is a drunk."

I said, "I know this, but she seems to care for you." He brushed it off and said he didn't want anything to do with that. For some strange reason, I felt like there was more to the story. I dropped it, though. He didn't want to talk about it, so neither did I.

Kassaundra had Travis doing a little bit of everything. As mentioned earlier, Travis was getting closer to becoming promoted to a general manager, so when we would have manager meetings, Kassaundra had Travis running part of it. Once we had a manager meeting and Travis came in to work but was not dressed for work. He was dressed casual with jeans and a sweater. He had his work clothes with him. They were hung up on a hanger. He proceeded to the office to get dressed; however, Maria saw him and asked to talk to him. They both went into the office and Travis closed the door. I noticed because I was on the cook line helping the cooks while Kassaundra and Franklin were out front helping the front of the house team. At first, I thought nothing of it, but it had been ten minutes and the office door was still shut.

A few minutes later, Travis and Maria came walking out of the office, but Travis had changed into his work clothes. I mean, he had on a different shirt and pants. How was this possible? Maria was in the office with him the entire time. And this office was very small. There was barely enough room for two people to fit. Now, I knew that Travis tried to play me like there was nothing going on, but who gets undressed in front of their employees? I knew at that moment something was going on between the two of them, but I left it alone. If one of the managers had walked into the office, I wondered what would've been seen.

For the meetings, Kassaundra would start the meeting and then she would let Travis take over. This is when you really saw the structured and militant style of Travis. Typically, manager meetings would be half informative and half venting sessions. Managers needed someone to vent to about how to deal with employees or guests. Well, Travis didn't want this to be a venting session. He kept everything clear and to the point. Franklin didn't like this and kept interrupting Travis. Travis seemed irritated with him, but he kept trying to stay focused. He looked as if he wanted to punch Franklin. Franklin knew this; however, he continued to harass him. It was like he had something on him. I bet you he knew about Travis and Maria. How could he not know? He and Maria were best friends.

I would continue to hang out with Travis, but he never once confided in me what was going on with him and Maria. I forgot about it because, like I said, he was juggling several women anyway. At one point, women he was dating started to come up to the restaurant to see him. I think he invited them to come because, conveniently, they would never come when Maria was working.

Once, he had three different ladies that he was talking to visit the restaurant at the same time. Luckily, we were very busy, so he was able to strategically place the women in different sections of the restaurant. He was sweating bullets, however, and asked me to run a little interference. He asked me to switch with him. I was initially running the kitchen and he was running the front. We switched and I went out front. He had me stop by the tables and check on the different ladies. He would pop out every few minutes to bring food out to a customer. He would grin and smile at other customers and then he would stop by and chitchat with one of his ladies. He gave the appearance that he talked to everyone so it wouldn't seem so obvious to one of the ladies if they saw him talking to anyone. He also used the excuse that we were really busy, and he was tied up in the kitchen. After he apologized for not being able to sit down with them, he would state that he really needed to get back to work. All three of the ladies stayed for over an hour, but to Travis it felt like they were there for ten hours. He was relieved when they all finally left. He said that he wasn't going to invite anyone that he was dating to his job anymore. I cried in laughter for the rest of the day! He even thought it was funny after the fact!

A few months later, Travis had slowly started to dwindle down his female friends. He told me that he couldn't continue at this pace. I laughed and said, "Well, there's always Maria!"

He laughed and said, "Like I told you before, that chick is a drunk."

He told me that he finally had someone he liked a lot and that she was different from all the other woman that he ever dated. I asked him what was different about this lady. He told me she was a police officer and that she was rising in the ranks. He stated this was good for their relationship because she worked a lot and stayed busy. He stated that he always stayed busy and didn't like women who were always underneath him and didn't have any life of their own. The most important part was, although he had been dating her for a while, they hadn't had sex or even come close to having sex. He told me that he respected her a lot for that.

He also said, "You won't believe this, but she is coming into the restaurant today to visit me."

I said, "Whoa, you remember what happened last time you had women coming in to visit you. I don't want no part of running interference again."

He laughed and assured me that he would not be utilizing my services this time. He said she would be the only one coming in to see him this time.

Around 8:30 that evening, Travis told me that she was here and that he wanted me to meet her. He was quite giddy about her being here. I told him I would be out in a few minutes. I cleaned myself up and came out to the dining room to find Travis and meet this lady he was giddy about. I came out to the dining room and didn't immediately see him, but I saw Simone and Mims at a table. That's when I saw Travis seated at a table across from his lady friend. Mims had a chair pulled up to the table. That was his thing. He always pulled a chair up to talk to someone, whether it was a good conversation or if he was going to escort you out of the restaurant. Travis's lady friend and Simone were laughing and conversing. Simone had that effect on everyone. I don't think there is a person alive who doesn't like the girl. She has a magnetic personality.

Anyhow, as I approached the table, Travis introduced me to his lady friend. I had to admit, she was gorgeous. I introduced myself to her. She introduced herself as Crystal. Not only was she gorgeous, but she was extremely polite. Travis was sitting there smiling like I had never seen before. Usually he was serious and reserved, but this was the first time I had ever seen him like this.

I told Travis I would take care of the restaurant for the rest of the evening and for him to just relax. He was grateful and went back to gazing at his new lady. As I walked away, Simone walked with me and stated that she had never seen Travis like this, and he seemed as if he was in love. I agreed with her. Mims walked up to me and Simone and said, "Oohh wee, our boy in love. I have never seen him acting like this before." Everyone seemed happy for Travis. I don't think anyone ever saw him smile or even act remotely relaxed.

Only one person was upset with Travis's new happiness and that was Maria. The other times one of Travis's lady friends came into the restaurant, Maria happened to not be at work. This time, however, she was. And she was not a happy camper. Although she was perceived as a tough cookie, this was too much for her. For the first time, she seemed vulnerable. I thought I was going to see her cry.

She never ended up crying, but she did whatever was possible to get Travis's attention. She continued to walk past the table that Travis was sitting at with his lady friend. Each time she walked by the table, Travis continued to ignore her. At one point, she brought a water over to the table even though water was never requested. Somehow, when Maria attempted to place the water down, she mistakenly misplaced it and the water fell in Crystal's lap. Crystal gasped with the shock of cold water in her lap and Travis jumped up to help her out. Maria tried to act as if it was a mistake and that she was sorry. We all knew it was no mistake and that she did that to get Travis's attention.

Well, she completely had Travis's attention. He had a look of fire in his eyes. Mims was back at the table in a hurry because he could tell by the look Travis was giving her that this was about to be a problem. All while Travis's lady friend wasn't looking, Mims grabbed Maria by the elbow and escorted her away from the table. Mims was always smooth and ahead of the situation.

Travis was right behind them. His lady friend quickly jogged up to Travis and gently placed her hand on his shoulder. He turned around and she could see the fire in his eyes. She told Travis that it was okay and that it was just an accident. She didn't want Maria to get in trouble for this simple mistake. She had no idea that Maria did this on purpose. Travis assured her that he wasn't going after the server but was going to get her some towels. He wasn't that convincing, and she noticed that. She calmly grabbed him by the hand and walked him back to the table.

Although Mims was not a manager, he told Maria that it was time for her to leave. Mims asked me if I could transfer her tables over to another server and get her out of the building as soon as possible. Mims knew what was going to happen once Travis got up from the table and he wanted to avoid any confrontations.

Maria also knew what was going to happen. Normally she would have something to say, but this time she swiftly got out of the building. I almost wanted Travis to get up before she left, but he probably would've lost his job. The entire time, Crystal thought it was a mistake.

Maria ended up calling off work for the rest of the week. This was a good thing, because Travis was still fuming for the next couple of days. She didn't return until the next week. By this time, Travis had calmed down but he still had nothing to say to her. She avoided him at all costs. This was a good thing! She was smarter than I thought she was.

Over the next couple of months, Travis stayed happy. He would often tell me about the wonderful times he had on his off days. He told me they were together the entire time that he was off. This was contradictory from what he said he initially wanted. He did not want to spend all his time with a woman. He confided in me that she was different and that he had not liked anyone like this for a long time. He said she was perfect. Her birthday was coming up and he was planning her a surprise birthday party. He invited me to come along.

He ended up renting out an entire club in the downtown Detroit area. It was impressive. The place was nice, and the music was slammin as well as the women at the party. Travis and his Crystal arrived about an hour after everyone else. I had found out that some of Travis's family as well as some of Crystal's family were already at the party. Once they walked in, we all shouted "Surprise!" She was completely surprised and bursted in tears of shock. She looked at Travis and gave him a big hug and a kiss. Travis was in heaven. I thought he was about to pop the question.

Travis spent the next few minutes walking around and

introducing her to some of the people that she didn't know. To my surprise, this was the first time Travis's family had met her. As he was introducing people, he also introduced me to a few of the people. I truly knew no one there. However, he ended up introducing me to his sister. Now, she was simply beautiful. I was instantly attracted. We connected almost immediately. I completely forgot that anyone else was at the party. We ended up dancing the night away. Only time we paused was when she had to go to the bathroom. When she left, I took a quick breather and got me a drink. It was getting late and some of the people had started to leave. I was kind of tired and ready to get her number and leave. I figured that she was tired as well and would be leaving soon also.

As soon as she walked back in the room, I was standing against the wall talking to Travis. I noticed his sister walk back into the room. She eyed me and beelined straight toward me, never taking her eyes off me. It was like no one else was in the room. She walked right up to me and still didn't take her eyes off me. She never looked at her brother. She was standing about six inches from me. I thought she was about to kiss me. She took the drink out of my hand and placed in on the bar. She grabbed my hand and seductively walked me back to the dance floor without ever taking her eyes off me. I heard Travis in the background say, "Well, damn, Sis!"

I couldn't believe it, but I was getting seduced and I was loving every moment of it. I think we danced nonstop for about another hour without our bodies ever separating. As the night was ending, Travis never did pop the question to his girlfriend as I expected, but I sure felt like popping the question to his sister. I was hooked.

We eventually ended our dancing as the lights came on and the music cut off. Sweating and slightly gasping for air, I realized that I had to go to the bathroom. I didn't want to leave her, but

I told her that I would be right back. I ran to the bathroom and when I came back, much to my surprise, she was gone. There was no trace of her. There were now only a few people left at the club and I knew none of them. I went and stood next to the women's bathroom. Assuredly she had to go to the bathroom again and would eventually come out. After about ten minutes, the bathroom door came open, but it wasn't her. I asked the lady coming out if there was someone else in the bathroom and she told me it was a single restroom and no one else was in there. I was deflated as I walked out the club. I thought maybe she was in the parking lot waiting for me, but there were no more cars. Feeling dejected, I got into my car and left. I couldn't believe this. We had such a great connection. I was sure that I was going to get her number. As I thought about it, I didn't even know her name. Damn!

The worst part of this was Travis was off for the rest of the week. I was dying to see him and ask him about his sister. I had to wait three more days until I saw him again. When we spoke, he thanked me for coming to the party. I told him I had a great time. Before he could say anything else, I asked him about his sister. I asked if she said anything about me the last few days. He told me that he spent the days with his girl and hadn't spoken to his sister. I told him that he should ask his sister if I could have her number. He looked at me and laughed. He told me that he doubted if she would ever call me because she had a boyfriend. I was shocked and said, "She didn't act like she had a boyfriend that night." I told him that we had a great connection.

I told him to ask her anyway. He shook his head in amusement and said, "Sure."

The next day when I saw Travis, I asked him what his sister's response was. He told me that, just as he told me the other day, she told him that she wasn't interested. She had a boyfriend and she was happy with him. They had a bad argument the day before and she broke up with him. Come to find out, the night of the party, when I went to the bathroom, she did indeed go outside to get some air. Travis told me that she was waiting for me to come out, but when she went outside her boyfriend was outside with some flowers waiting for her. He said that he didn't come into the party because he didn't want to make a scene. She ended up leaving with him on the spot. I was floored, because I was really into her.

Travis and I continued to hang out over the next few months, but I never brought up his sister again. I was low-key still a little upset about it. He never brought her name up either. I would end up seeing her again. On a Sunday after church, Travis's family came into the Blue Crab to have lunch. Of course, his sister was with the family. She looked just as good as she did on the night of the party. I stopped by and said hello to the family. His parents were cordial, but his sister acted as if she had never seen me a day in her life. I found myself a little irritated, so I kindly excused myself and walked off.

Surprisingly, the more me and Travis hung out, the less he spoke about Crystal. At first, I didn't think nothing of it, but it became noticeable after some time. When I asked about her, he would say, "She good." I stopped asking about her and he stopped talking about her. Eventually, he told me that they broke up. He said she was too much into her career. He also stated that with her being a female officer in a male-dominated field, she had to be around men too much. She was constantly on the phone with her male partner or talking to her police lieutenant who was also a man. I think Travis was a little jealous because he was a control freak and couldn't control this lady. I was a little sad for him because she seemed to be a great lady and he was missing out.

Mims

Mims was as cool as they come. Mims was not only our security, but he was our voice of reason. Every manager respected Mims, including Kassaundra. Having Mims working was like having another manager on duty. Oftentimes we would all get his advice on something, whether it was personal or business-related. I think the crew respected Mims more than they respected the managers. Mims would joke sometimes that he should be a manager. He swore that he could whip this place into shape if he was the general manager. I believed him as well. Only thing, we all knew that Mims would never be a manager. He was a head foreman at one of the biggest plants in Detroit. Being a manager would be a pay cut and more hours for him. He mentioned that he only did security to set up his two boys who were in college. He said that he didn't touch any of the money from the plant to cover his boys. He used his side gig to take care of all their needs, so his retirement was never in question. Smart man.

Mims carried himself well and he didn't play no games. He was always aware of any situation and would never be too far away. Mims, despite being older than all of us, was quite the ladies' man. On nights that he would work security, he would always have some young thangs meet him and hang out at the restaurant. All the guys would be impressed because he was pulling girls our age that we should've been pulling. He was cool about it as well. He never bragged or made a scene; he was just cool! Our female customers were also fair game to Mims. He never went after them, but they always found a way to strike up conversation.

What made it even better for Mims was that he could sing very well. We found this out one day when the servers were singing "Happy Birthday" to one of the guests. This guest happened to be one of the ladies who was already flirting with Mims earlier. Once the servers walked away from the table, Mims walked over and pulled a chair up. He started to serenade her. The restaurant stopped because Mims sounded like Teddy Pendergrass. If he was on stage, I swear the lady would've thrown panties at him. After he was through singing, the lady wrote her number down on a napkin and handed it to him. For the rest of the night, the crew asked him to sing to their guests. All the servers received bigger tips because of his singing.

This wasn't the only time Mims would pull a chair up. Any time that we had an irate customer that either refused to pay for their bill or refused to leave, we would send Mims over to the table. There were plenty of times the customers would be irate with us, but Mims had a way of smoothing things over. It wasn't because he had a gun either.

His gun was concealed, and Mims never wore a security uniform. He always dressed in plain clothes and was very dapper. When he approached the table, he always looked like someone's dad instead of security, which set people at ease.

Most of the ladies he was able to win over with his charisma. The guys he would just be real with them but firm. He would treat them like men but would not bend on the decision that the managers made. Some of the guys would try to act tough and speak over Mims, but he knew how to handle that, too. He would never back down from them, but he was firm with them.

On one occasion, we sent Mims to go talk to this guest who was rude to not only the servers but also to the managers. This guy was angry that his food took a long time to come out. Once it did come out, he cursed at the server and told her that she was a slow-ass bitch. This was a no-no! We never allowed our guests to talk to anyone in this manner.

Once this was brought to our attention, Franklin went to the table to talk to the guy.

Franklin had no tact and asked the customer straight up, "Did you just call one of my servers a slow-ass bitch?"

The guy was just as hood as Franklin. He looked at him and said, "Yeah, bitch, I called your server a bitch."

Franklin said, "Aw hell no, you got to leave this restaurant right now."

The customer laughed and said that he wasn't going nowhere. Franklin spent no time going to get Mims. Once Mims came over and tried to talk to the customer, the customer said, "Nigga, you can walk away too! I already told that bitch nigga that I ain't going nowhere."

Mims kept his cool and still pulled up a chair. He told the customer, "Hey, brother, I can feel that you are upset, but you are handling this all wrong. This is a family establishment and we got kids in this place. You can't be talking like that up in here. Now the manager asked you kindly to leave, so I suggest that you just leave. We aren't asking for money for what you already ate, they just want you to go."

The customer once again told Mims, "Nigga, like I said before, you can just walk away."

Mims said, "No problem, brother, if this the way you want to handle this." Mims got up and walked away. He went to the kitchen and talked to Franklin. He told him to go ahead and call the police. Mims hated getting the police involved. Firstly, he felt like he could handle any situation and, secondly, he truly didn't want a customer to get arrested.

For whatever reason, when Mims went into the kitchen to talk to Franklin, the customer must have felt offended or threatened. The customer got up and walked right into the kitchen to confront Mims.

Mims was shocked that the guy walked into the kitchen and told him, "Hey, brother, you got to get out of here!"

Now Mims was not a small guy. He was about six feet tall and stocky, but this customer had to be about six feet five inches with muscles practically popping out of his shirt.

The customer walked up to Mims and said, "I should fuck you up for trying to embarrass me out there."

Mims was calm as he said, "My man, first you got about three minutes to get out of here before the cops arrive. Second of all, if you want to bring it, then bring it. I'm always ready! Keep in mind you got about two and a half minutes now. My question for you: are you straight? You ain't got no warrants out on you, do you? I can see that you trying to conceal that gun you got in your waistline. That gun clean? Probably got a little weed on you too, right, brother?"

Mims must've been correct on everything, because the guy paused as if he was thinking about everything. The guy looked at Mims and said, "My bad, bro, you right. I could've handled things differently. I sure don't want to deal with the police and end up back in jail. Good lookin out, bro."

He then pulled cash out of his pocket and handed it to Mims. He said that it should cover the bill plus a tip. The customer hurried up and got out of there. Mims was still cool, but he later said, "That dude was out of his mind. I thought that I was going to have to shoot him."

ALL YOU CAN EAT

Every year in September, the Blue Crab would run their most famous promotion: All You Can Eat crab legs. The company loved this promotion and they spent a lot of time promoting it. A ton of commercials and email blasts ensured everyone knew about it. I understood the methodology behind the AYCE (All You Can Eat). September was a normally slow time of the year for restaurants. This promotion helped bring in guests that normally would not come in.

As a management team, we tried our best to show enthusiasm for the promotion, but it would be to no avail. The Blue Crab had been running this promo for years. Everyone knew this promotion sucked. We all hated this promotion. AYCE for only $13.99 per person. It was a cheap promotion that tended to bring out the worst of the worst customers.

The customers rarely ordered anything else besides the crab legs, so our check average would always be low. There was no up-selling. They were not going to order drinks, appetizers, or dessert. Besides the tips being terrible, they would constantly run you. The customers would eat the crab legs faster than you could go back and get more. Typically, when people eat crab legs, they try to get every single morsel of meat out of it. You would even see people sucking the meat out of the smaller legs. People wanted to get their money's worth. However, with AYCE our guests wouldn't try that hard to get all of the meat out; they would just toss it to the side and order more crab.

Also, because it was All You Can Eat, the last-minute stragglers that came in just before closing still had up to an hour after closing to get more crab legs. The kitchen crew would be furious because they couldn't begin cleaning up. Everyone that worked here would leave at the end of their shift smelling like stinky crab legs. You just couldn't avoid it.

Although all advertisements on television and the menu said All You Can Eat per person, it never mattered with the difficult guests at this location. Servers hated it because people would never get up. They could not get new tables because people would sit longer ordering more crab legs. It was gluttony at its worst. They were always trying to get over on us. We had to instruct the servers to let every guest know that the promotion was per person.

They also had to inform the guests they couldn't bring any takeout boxes to the table until they were done eating. Once a takeout box was on the table, the managers would not allow servers to bring any more crab legs. We instructed the servers on this every single shift. Although we instructed the servers on this, people would still try to share.

This night would be no different. We had a lot of terrible guests that came; however, we had one family that was the worst. It was four women and three small children, and they were ridiculous! First, they just ordered water and no appetizers. They told the server that only two of them were going to eat and they were going to get the All You Can Eat crab. We all knew that was a lie.

The server politely informed them this promotion was per

person and there was no sharing allowed. The guests, of course, said no problem. They informed the server that the other guests and the kids had already eaten and were just hanging out with them. Again, we all knew this was a lie.

As soon as the crab legs came out, everyone at the table started to dig in. The server mentioned to the guests again that the All You Can Eat was only per person and they couldn't share. One of the ladies at the table said, "No problem, they all just wanted to try one crab leg." This was again a lie because everyone kept eating. The customers continued to order more crab legs, and everyone continued to eat. The server brought this to my attention and asked if I could stop by the table and speak with them.

I immediately headed over to the table and introduced myself to the family. The family seemed agitated that I had stopped by. Before I could say another word, one of the ladies interrupted and said, "We know, we know. No sharing! We already told the server that we ain't sharing. The kids just wanted to try one leg and that is all. Is that a problem?"

I told them that it wasn't a problem that the kids tried one crab leg, but it was to my understanding that everyone at the table was sharing every time we brought more crab legs. They told me this was not true, and they weren't sharing. They must have thought I was a fool. There were crab shells in front of everyone as well as remnants of crab meat everywhere. I didn't want to fight with the ladies, so I simply stated that I was glad they were here, and I appreciated them for not sharing. I apologized for interrupting and stated that we had a problem with people sharing and not wanting to pay for it. They assured me that they were not sharing.

The server was furious with me for not being more forceful with this group. I told the server that I had it under control and to just take care of her guests. Over the next half hour, I kept an eye on the table and no one else was eating crab legs except for the two ladies. The server seemed to chill out because they were not sharing any longer, but she said that she couldn't believe how much these ladies were eating. What myself and the server didn't realize was that the table was asking other servers to go and get them a box. We had no idea they were doing this until another server came in the kitchen and said that this table kept asking them for boxes every time they walked by.

So, I decided to walk the next order of crab legs to the table myself. I dropped it off and didn't say anything. I walked away and went and stood out of their eyesight. I noticed that as soon as they couldn't see me, one of the ladies dumped the crab legs into her purse. Yes, I did say her purse. I never saw anything like this in my life. I hurriedly got over to the table before she could close her purse up. I had walked from a different direction because I noticed they had the whole table on alert looking in the direction of the kitchen. When they noticed that I or their server wasn't around, they would dump the crab legs. When I approached from behind them, I noticed they had their purse lined with plastic wrap. There was nothing in the purse but crab legs. I was dumbfounded. I also noticed that they had five boxes hidden under their table full of crab legs. The crab legs were all sticking out of the box. Just as I was about to say something, one of the ladies finally noticed me and it startled her.

She instantly closed her purse shut and said, "Hello, how you doing!"

She said this with so much attitude and was instantly on the defensive. The other ladies started clutching their purses as well. I had no doubt they all had crab legs in their purses.

I advised the ladies that we would no longer bring anymore crab legs to the table. One of the ladies had the audacity to say, "Well, we aren't done eating."

I advised them they were indeed done eating here.

They were beside themselves and stated, "This is false promotion. Your advertisement says All You Can Eat."

I retorted, "Yeah, but not all you can take home."

I was done playing with the ladies and told them so. "Listen, ladies, just let it go. I am already aware that you all have crab legs in your purses as well as five boxes under the table full of crab legs. Just call it a day, you've won, but not another crab leg will be coming to your table," I stated.

I left their bill on the table and said that we would take payment whenever they were ready. They wouldn't leave it alone, however. They told me they did not have crab legs in their purse and the boxes were from the other restaurant they had just ate at. It almost sounded believable for how fat they were.

"Listen, ladies, you can either pay for the two meals and leave or I will charge the table for all seven orders of All You Can Eat crab legs that you all ate. I also will not bring more crab legs until you eat what is in your boxes under the table," I replied.

They were enraged at my comment and said they were offended by me questioning them. They wanted to know my name, my boss's name, and the number to our corporate office. They also said they weren't going to pay for anything since I offended them like this. I wasn't going to argue with them about their pettiness.

I told them, "Look, either pay your bill or take it up with the police."

They were now even more furious and said they are leaving and that I would be getting fired for this. I walked away from the table and told Mims what was going on. He asked me to hold off on calling the police and said he was sure he could handle it.

Mims stopped by the table and pulled up a chair. I overheard him talking to the ladies, but they were just getting louder. He eventually got them to calm down, but they said they still weren't going to pay for anything. Mims pleaded with them to pay. He advised them that if the manager called the police, they were going to have to pay for it anyway. He even explained to them that I was being easy on them for not charging them for everything they ate. They didn't want to hear a word that he was saying. They just said they were not going to pay, and that the manager would be getting fired for this. He pleaded with them again, but to no avail. He shrugged and simply got up from the table.

Mims walked over to me and said, "Do what you got to do, these ladies said they aren't going to pay for anything. I couldn't talk them out of it." Unlike Mims, I didn't care if they got arrested. These ladies were a ridiculous bunch and were doing too much. I walked away from Mims and called the police. As soon as I hung up with the police, I noticed the ladies were walking toward the lobby. I immediately stopped by the table to see if they had left some money. There was no money on the table, so I ran and asked the server if the customers gave her any money. She said they hadn't. I raced to the front to attempt to get their payment.

Mims saw me moving and he was right behind me. We got to the ladies just as they were exiting the building. Mims told them they must pay for this bill. Two of the ladies kept walking and the other two with the children stopped. They started arguing toward me and stating that I was unprofessional in the manner I handled this. Mims told them once again they must pay. Just as the ladies started arguing with Mims, the police pulled up. The policemen got out of their car and started toward us. They knew exactly where they were heading because the two ladies were still cursing and yelling.

Just as the police approached, the ladies gathered the kids and started walking away. The ladies walked right passed them. The police sensed that something wasn't right, so they asked the ladies to stop. The ladies kept walking. This pissed the police officers further. One of the officers yelled at them to stop immediately. The ladies stopped and started yelling at the officers. The officers yelled back, telling them to quiet down. The other two ladies who had originally made it to their car came back to join their friends in the argument. Mims and I were just looking at each other in awe. Two of the ladies were so enraged, they were literally six inches from the police officers' faces.

One of the police officers put his hand and pushed one of the ladies away. He yelled at her to calm down. Once that happened, she pointed her finger in his face and yelled, "This is police brutality!" This was a huge mistake, because next thing we know she was slammed face first into the ground. One of her sisters was thrown down just as fast. As they were thrown down, their purses went sprawling everywhere and so did the crab legs that were in them. There were crab legs everywhere. Another one of the sisters jumped on the officer to try to get him off her and she was quickly face planted onto the cement as well.

The police ended up calling for back-up to haul the three ladies away. Once things calmed down, the remaining sister who was with the children began to talk to the officers. She was pleading with them to not take her sisters away. They were not interested in her plea.

Finally, the arresting officers asked me what happened. I forgot that we never had a chance to speak because the ladies had become belligerent as soon as the police showed up. I told them what happened and that the ladies refused to pay the bill. The police asked if I had the bill and I told them that I would have to retrieve it from inside. Now this was a lie. I had the original bill on me, but I had only charged them for the two All You Can Eat meals. Since I was going back inside, I was going to charge them for the seven that I had threatened them with. I didn't feel bad about it either, because they truly ordered this amount.

When I came back out outside, I handed the police officer the check. He handed the check to the remaining sister.

She yelled, "Oh, I only had one order. We had separate checks. The rest of this is their bill, but you arrested them. I'm only going to pay for my meal."

The police officer yelled back at her and said, "Y'all came together, so y'all pay together."

She refused to pay for the rest of the check. The officer informed her that she could either pay for the entire check or she could get arrested too. He also stated that he could call the Department of Family and Children Services to take the children. She instantly paid for the entire check and left.

I was relieved to have the situation over. As the police were pulling off, I could see the women in the back of the cruiser. They were crying, but I felt no remorse for them. I laughed and we walked back into the building. This made the night for everyone, including myself. Simone even was laughing and said, "Look at you, Carter, the Blue Crab superhero." She gave me a hug and whispered to me again that this was sexy. Once again, I was turned on, but I had to play it cool and get away from her.

The only person that wasn't happy was the server. She was upset that she spent all that time bringing crab legs to the table and she didn't receive a tip. I ended up splitting off two of the meals and comping it. This way she was able to receive some of the money. I wasn't supposed to do this, but I thought it was the right thing to do for our server. I was happy that someone paid for acting like an idiot.

Truthfully, if they would've just paid and got home and called the corporate office, they would've most likely received either reimbursement or gift cards. Our corporate office always gave way to the guests, even if the guests were wrong. The Blue Crab just wanted to keep every customer. I don't think every customer is worth keeping, if they are scammers or cause other customers to not want to visit your locale. After this incident, I think Mims stopped feeling empathy for our guests. His comment was that if they wanted to come out and act a fool, that was their problem. He said he wasn't concerned about their well-being any longer and they could just go to jail.

I couldn't wait for this promotion to be over.

* * *

At our manager meeting, Kassaundra told us to be on the lookout for not only the terrible guests during this promotion, but also our crew. She told us that the crew always stole during this promotion and that someone always got fired for this.

That same evening, Franklin and I were working when a server tried to get a scam over on us. I was working out front and didn't notice the scam. However, Franklin was in the kitchen working when he noticed. The only reason he noticed was that it was a server named Tabitha that he couldn't stand. Franklin was trying to get her fired. Tabitha had complained to Kassaundra about Franklin on several occasions. It didn't matter what anyone else did, but if Tabitha did something wrong, Franklin was all over it.

Well this night, Franklin noticed that Tabitha had an excessive amount of crab legs going out to the tables. Tabitha, who was never around to walk food to a table, even her own, was right there every time her food came up. Franklin thought this was a little strange and went into investigation mode. Franklin found out from Maria that Tabitha's family was here eating dinner. He had me walk past the table to see what they had. He didn't want to walk past it and seem so obvious.

Next, we pulled up Tabitha's order on the computer to see what was rung up. To our surprise, there was only one entrée rang up, but there were four people eating. Tabitha continued to ring up refill orders on that one meal for additional crab legs to come out. Each person had a least four clusters of crab legs sitting in front of them.

Franklin looked at me and smiled.

He said, "I finally got this bitch. Caught her ass red-handed."

She was indeed caught red-handed.

Franklin wasted no time pulling Tabitha to the side. Tabitha knew that she was caught and tried to lie about it. She said she was going to ring in everything later, but she was just trying to get all the crab legs as quick as possible. Franklin stood there smiling at her. He was enjoying this.

Franklin said, "Naw, you were stealing. You know that you got to ring it, then bring it. You got to go."

Tabitha insisted that she was not stealing and asked for

Kassaundra's number. Franklin told her that Kassaundra wasn't available and that he was running the store tonight. Tabitha tried to argue with Franklin and make a scene, but Mims came around and politely escorted Tabitha out the building.

You Can Run, But You Can't Hide

At the Blue Crab, we had a rule for servers and bartenders: If you have more than one walk-out, you will be removed from any cash handling position. A walk-out meant not collecting payment from a guest before they left. Although servers hated this rule, it prevented the Blue Crab from losing any money and held the server accountable. We expected them to collect all payments from the guests unless the guests were physically running out the building. Again, the reason to have security at this location.

We had several different security personnel that would alternate the nights they worked. They were all very good, but Mims was always two steps ahead, preventing situations before they got out of hand. Luckily, Mims was working this particular night!

Mims was sitting in the lobby, chatting with Simone. As they were talking, two guys swiftly exited the building. This caught Mims's attention. Mims ended his conversation with Simone and started toward the door. Just then, a server came running up with an empty bill fold. He said these two guys just ran out without paying. He said they asked him for dessert and just as he was entering the kitchen, he noticed the guys heading toward the lobby.

Mims went outside to see if he could catch them, but they were running. Before we knew it, Mims ran and jumped into his car. Mims was gone for about thirty minutes and we didn't know what was going on. We tried calling him, but he was not answering his phone. We were worried about him. Once the guests left the premises, we were not to go after them under any circumstances. I guess Mims figured this didn't apply to him because he was security. After a few more minutes, Mims came walking back into the building and he was smiling.

I was a little freaked out and asked Mims was everything okay. There was about ten of us standing in the lobby and everyone wanted to know what happened. He walked over to the server and gave him a stack of cash. The server was relieved because the money covered the entire check as well as a great tip. Mims was enjoying this moment as he was grinning ear to ear.

He explained that when he first went outside, he was going to catch the guys before they got into their cars, except they didn't get into their cars. They ran down the street. He stated that this is when he jumped into his car and decided to follow them. He said he was originally going to see where they went and call the police, but the guys ended up going into the gas station at the corner. They were laughing and giving each other high-fives as they entered the gas station. The guys never noticed that Mims was following them. Mims said he assessed the situation and realized the guys were just some young punks. He didn't want these guys to go to jail, but he did want to scare them a little bit.

Mims stated that he quietly slipped into the gas station. He knew the gas station owners because he would often stop there to get gas or snacks for himself. The gas station owners liked when Mims stopped by because he would have his security shield hanging around his neck and his gun would be on his hip. It was funny because Mims had never shown his badge or gun at the restaurant. Mims said that he did this if he had to go to the gas station at night. We were in the hood and he didn't want any issues. Most people figured he was a cop because his shield resembled a cop's. He also carried himself with swagger as if he were the law, so most people would never question the badge.

As Mims slipped into the gas station, he quietly locked the door behind him. The owners noticed but the two young guys hadn't. Mims looked at the owners and discreetly put one finger up to his lips and signaled *shush*. At this point, the guys were walking back toward the front swiftly with a couple of bags of chips and some beer in their hands. They were intending to run out of there without paying as well. As they got closer to the door, they sprinted at full speed. They had no idea the door was locked but were soon about to find out. The lead guy ran so fast toward the door, not realizing that it was locked, that he completely faced planted into the door. The door hit him with so much force that he was instantly knocked out. As he crumpled toward the floor, his partner paused in shock. Just as the partner was about to try the door, Mims tapped him on the shoulder. The guy turned around defensively but stopped abruptly when he saw Mims's pistol looking directly at him.

As Mims was looking at him, he noticed these were just two young guys that had no business out here trying to do wrong. He lowered the gun and told the young man to relax. It was too late, however, as Mims noticed a yellowish fluid on the floor by his feet. The young man had peed on himself.

Mims put his gun back in the holster. The young man was in tears now as he looked at Mims. Mims told the young man that he hoped they had money to pay for this because they were about to go to jail if not. As he was saying this, the other guy was waking up.

The other guy quickly realized they were in trouble. He tried to get up quickly to make a mad dash, but Mims was a step ahead of him. As they guy tried to push himself up, Mims drove the heel of his dress shoes into the back of his hand. The guy yelled out in pain. Mims told him to just stay on the floor and relax. He knew not to move, but as he was getting his bearings he looked around and saw his buddy standing there with Mims. His buddy's pants were wet and there was yellow liquid on the floor. He pushed himself away quickly, but he already had pee on him from his buddy. He tried to get up, but Mims told him to stay there. The guy said, "Man, I don't want to sit here in some piss!"

Mims looked at him and put his hand on his hip, exposing his gun. Mims looked at him and said, "You will be my wet floor sign for now. Don't move." The guy didn't move.

Mims explained to them that he was security for the Blue Crab and that he just observed them running out without paying. He told him that he wanted the money for the entire check plus tip or he was handing them over to the police. He also said they needed to pay for the items they were running out with at this gas station. Wet-floor-sign dude went into his pocket and pulled out a wad of money. He looked at Mims and said, "Man, I am sorry, here is the money but please don't call the police. I am so sorry." He handed over the money to Mims. Mims slowly counted the money and once he realized it was all there, he unlocked the door and let the guys go. Mims went and paid the gas station owners and then walked out and got into his car.

I doubted if we would ever see those two guys again.

Knock Your Head Off

I was grateful that we had Mims. He surely saved us from disaster quite a few times. On one occasion particularly, he saved my job. On this evening, we were extremely busy. Our dining room was full and so was our anchor. This was just a regular Tuesday night. We were typically slow on Mondays and Tuesdays, even at night. We never opened our anchor room until the weekend nights, but this night we had to. Our dining room was full, and we had two different birthday parties of thirty people each. I was able to accommodate both parties in the anchor.

I had the host separate the room and put each party on separate sides of the room. After they were seated, someone from one of the parties asked to see the manager. Both parties were upset they had to wait a long time to be seated once they saw that we had all this room in the anchor. The party on the left side was a little more reserved than the party on the right side.

As I was talking to the party on the left side, the party on the right side started yelling for me. I told the party that I would be right with them as soon as I was finished talking to the other table. They didn't want to hear this and kept yelling over for me. I ended up addressing both parties at the same time. I told them once again that I apologized for the wait and that I would bring out several appetizers for both parties.

This seemed to have calmed everyone except for one guy on the right side of the room. He shouted out this wasn't going to be enough and that he wanted a few more appetizers. Although I didn't want to give in, I went ahead and conceded. Well, as soon as I did this the left side of the room asked for me again. They stated that since I gave the other guests a few more appetizers, they should receive the same compensation. I was fuming inwardly but I conceded with them because they were waiting the same amount of time.

Over the next hour, things started to slow down and get back to normal. I went into the kitchen and helped get the food out for the large parties. I avoided the parties because I didn't want them to ask me for more freebies. Just as I thought I was going to be able to avoid them completely, one of my servers came to me and told me I was needed by one of the guests of the large parties. I gritted my teeth and headed to the anchor. We had two servers on each party, so I wanted to find the servers first and ask them which guest wanted me. I wanted to be able to isolate and speak with this guest alone without speaking to the entire party. This way if there was an issue, I could take care of this single issue without having everyone at both parties try to milk me for a freebie.

However, as I entered the anchor, there was no server to be found. I attempted to keep going and exit the room to find the servers, but once again the guy on the right side of the room yelled out for me.

He said, "Yo, my man! Didn't one of your waitresses say we needed to see a manager?"

I told him, "Yes, they did tell me this, but because no server was back here, I wanted to go find out which guest needed me. I didn't want to interrupt everyone's conversation. My apologies, but I'm assuming that it is you who needed me!"

The rude customer shouted out, "Bullshit, you were just trying to ignore me."

I was instantly on the defensive, but I was able to reel in my emotions.

I gathered myself and stated to the guy, "Sir, I definitely apologize for the mishap; however, I am going to ask you to refrain from using profanity toward me in the restaurant."

Now, everyone started talking to me at once. I knew that everyone was going to try to milk me for everything. I was able to recapture the room and told everyone that I would be more than happy to speak to everyone, but it would be one at a time.

Just as everyone calmed down, the rude customer yelled out, "We want everything to be for free!"

I told him that I would not be able to buy the entire bill, but I would try to do something for him.

He then stood up and shouted, "I don't give a fuck what you do for everyone else, but me and my family are not going to pay for anything."

I was taken aback and stated more aggressively, "Sir, I asked you once to not use profanity. This is a family restaurant."

He said, "I don't give a fuck!"

I quickly caught myself because I almost repeated the same sentiment back to him.

I barked, "Sir, I already advised you to not speak to me in this manner and that we are a family restaurant. Obviously, you didn't get it. At this point, there is nothing I am willing to do for you. If you like, you can call our corporate office, but I will not be speaking to you any further."

I walked away from him and went to speak to another guest on the other side of the room. This must've really pissed him off, because he stood up and yelled, "Nigga, I ain't done talking to you!"

I looked at him and said, "Well, I am done talking to you!"

He started walking in my direction and swinging his right arm side to side. He had a cast on his left foot, so he was limping as he was walking toward me. As he was walking toward me, he was looking at me and said, "Nigga, I'm about to knock your motherfuckin' head off."

I didn't say another word, but I stood there waiting for him to get closer. I knew that my management career was over and at this point I didn't care. There was no way I was going to let this dude swing on me. I was calculating the moment he got into my arm distance that I was going to start swinging on him. I knew he was the type of guy who wanted to get in my face and yell first. I was going to catch him slipping and then I was going to stomp on his already injured foot. I knew his family was going to jump me, but I was going to smash him first.

Just as the guy was getting closer and I was about to swing on him, I heard a voice over my shoulder saying, "I wouldn't do that if I were you!" The guy stopped in his tracks as Mims was standing behind me with his shield out. Mims told him to turn around and sit down. The guy looked at me as if he was going to still do something. Mims stood in front of me and told the guy, "Go ahead, I dare you!" The guy thought about it and then turned around. Mims looked at me and said, "Carter, I got it from here! Let me talk to them."

As I walked away, I started shaking again. I was not shaking when I thought my job was about to be over. Why was I shaking now? I was glad that Mims was here this evening. He was able to get the money from everyone and have them leave. I stayed in the back until they left. I was disgusted with myself for shaking. I just didn't get it. Thank God for Mims, however. If he wasn't there, I would have been unemployed.

TEACHING ME LESSONS

Although I had started to develop a pretty solid relationship with Franklin and Travis, Kassaundra and I rarely spoke. To be honest, I couldn't stand her, and I think she didn't care too much for me either. She was the type of person who led by fear and intimidation, whereas I liked to coach and develop. I felt that she spoke down to me the few times that we talked. I tried to have her teach me things regarding our profit and loss statements, but she was always too busy. The few times she did sit down with me, she had the same teaching style as Travis. She didn't understand why I didn't get it. I stopped asking her questions and leaned toward Franklin showing me something instead of her.

I truly believed she was upset with getting a brand new manager. She was already a first-time general manager at a rough location and then to send her a brand new manager that knew nothing about management was tough. However, instead of teaching me, she always seemed to just get angry at me. She would always teach me lessons instead of just teaching me.

One of my shifts that I worked with her, I was what you called a mid-shift manager. This meant I would come in at noon and not leave until we locked the doors at 10:00 p.m. I hated this shift!

Your day was wasted. You really didn't have time for yourself in the morning because you were already getting ready for work at 10:30 a.m. You also didn't have time to do anything after work either. I tried my best to never work these shifts if I could help it.

To make it worse, it was a busy Sunday and Kassaundra was the closer. Once she came in, I worked the front of the restaurant and she worked the kitchen. We had hardly conversed about anything the entire evening. She came in with an attitude, as usual, and I just wanted to stay away. I was glad that it was busy because it made time go by faster. As the night sped forward, I was getting happy as I anticipated getting out of here.

I waited a few minutes after closing and said my goodbyes to everyone. Then I went to Kassaundra and asked if she needed anything from me before I left for the evening.

She scowled and said, "No!" without even looking at me.

"All right, goodbye!" I replied.

I should've just left, but as I was leaving one of our servers asked me to remove something off a bill. I did that as quickly as possible and beelined to the front door. I was almost out of the door when Kassaundra called out to me. "Hey, Carter!"

I instantly regretted that I hadn't left yet. "Yes?" I replied.

"Did you do invoices?" she asked.

Now, I had been working here for a few months and I had yet to do an invoice. Matter of fact, I hadn't done an invoice since I was in training. Even then, I had only done a couple, and that was with guidance from another manager.

Reluctantly, I replied, "No, I didn't."

"Well, how are you expecting to go anywhere and you haven't done the invoices? I hope you didn't think that I was going to do all of them!"

"Um, no, ma'am! I just forgot to do them. I can come in early tomorrow morning and do them if you like," I said nervously.

Truth is, I knew Franklin would be working in the morning and he could show me how to do the invoices. Plus, I was tired. She knew I had no idea how to do the invoices.

"No, they have to be completed on Sunday night. The invoices go out on Monday morning and I have to second approve them all. You need to get in here and get them done," she barked.

I was agitated, but I went into the office to get them done. I had to remember how to do them first. I got in front of the computer and realized that I had forgotten how to do them completely. I attempted to call Franklin, but he didn't answer his phone. I then went back on our back-office system and attempted to do the tutorial on how to do invoices. I clicked on that and it said that the tutorial was twenty minutes long. *OMG*, I thought. I was going to be here all night! I watched the tutorial and then attempted to do the invoices.

These invoices were nothing like the examples they showed on the tutorial. I truly had no idea what I was doing. It didn't help that there were more than twenty invoices that needed to be completed. I fumbled through and had gotten about five of them done when Kassaundra walked into the office. It was almost an hour after she asked me to do them.

"Are you done yet?" she barked.

Again, I started with the shaking. "Not yet! I only did five of them so far," I replied.

"You've been in this office for over an hour and that's all you have done? It should've taken you no more than twenty minutes to get these done," she stated. "Listen, I don't want to be in here all night. Stay logged in and I will complete the invoices."

Relieved, I said, "Sorry that it was taking me so long, I haven't done invoices since training. Maybe you could show me how to do them a little quicker?"

Kassaundra replied, "No, thank you! I don't have time to be teaching you anything right now. Like I said, I don't want to be here all night."

"Okay, well can I go home now?" I asked.

She looked at me as if she could murder me and said, "No, you can't go home. Since I am doing the invoices for you, you can go and count the money. Like I said before, I'm not going to be here all night."

I went out front and counted the money, but I had an attitude. When I was done, I didn't do anything else. I just waited for her to be done. About twenty minutes later, she came out and said that she was done. She told me that I could leave. *If it took her that short of time to do them, she could've shown me how to do it as well,* I thought. However, I grabbed my things and ran out of there before she could ask me anything else.

★ ★ ★

Another shift that I worked with her, we were both closing. When it was getting closer to close, she told me that I would check everyone out and that she would do all the money. This was no problem with me. I was used to checking people out. I had closed plenty of times by myself. Checking people out meant that I had to look at every component of their area and make sure it was clean before they left. In the front of the house, I would be looking for cleanliness of tables, floors, and walls. In the kitchen, it would be the same, with food rotation and labeling added.

Checking people out would be a piece of cake. Since Kassaundra was counting the money, I rushed everyone to get done so that we could be out of here quickly. Most people loved closing with me because I was the quickest manager to get everyone out of here at night. They complained when it was the other managers. The crew stated that I got out of here an hour earlier than all the other managers.

Tonight, I was going to show Kassaundra that I was good at something. About forty minutes after close, I had the entire restaurant shut down, with the exception of the dishwashers. Kassaundra was still counting money, so I went to her to see if she needed help with anything. I told her that everyone was out except for the dishwashers. She raised her eyebrow and said, "Everyone is gone?"

Proudly, I said, "Yep, except for the dishwashers and they will be done in five minutes."

As Kassaundra was counting money, she shook her head as if she didn't believe me that everyone was done. She was doubting my abilities. A few minutes later, I went back and checked out the dish guys. They were just finishing up when I came back. I told them all was good, and they could clock out and go home. I went back up front and talked to Mims.

It was only me, Mims, and Kassaundra left in the building. It took Kassaundra about thirty more minutes to get done. By the time she was done, I had all the lights in the restaurant cut off, with my keys in my hand. I was ready to go!

Just when I thought Kassaundra was about to come out the back, I noticed that all of the lights started coming back on in the restaurant. She came out front looking mad as ever! "Carter, did you check everyone out?" She scowled.

Confused, I said, "Yes."

"Well, let's take a walk around the restaurant," she demanded.

We started off walking the front of the restaurant. I got it— she wanted to check me out to see if I checked the crew out. As we were walking around, she broke a flashlight out of her pocket. She flashed the light under every table. Almost every table had some debris toward the back of the table. She looked at me angrily and said, "I thought you said you checked out everyone." I had nothing to say. She said nothing either as she handed me the carpet sweeper. I knew this meant that she wanted me to clean under the booths. I hated that I missed it, because some of the tables had broken crab shells under the table. I couldn't get these with the sweeper, so I had to pick these up by hand. There was also gum stuck under three tables that I had to get up as well. We had a scraper that we used just for gum, but I couldn't find it. I had to use paper towel to get it. It was disgusting.

Once I was done getting through cleaning under the booths, she showed me four tables that hadn't been wiped down properly. I couldn't believe that I hadn't seen this. I had to clean those as well.

Once I completed those, she motioned for me to follow her to the kitchen. I followed her to the kitchen and she instantly started pulling the under-counter refrigerators from the wall. "Look at all that crap under there!" she said as she pointed to piles of debris that weren't swept. "You need to go and get the broom and dustpan and clean all of this up. Afterward, get the mop bucket and mop all this crap up. Once you are done with that, the dish area is a mess. The inside of the dish machine needs to be cleaned out as well. The floors need to be re-mopped. Lastly, all the trash by the back door needs to be tied up, covered, and organized. Get that done and come back and get me so that I can check it out."

I got everything done and complete, but it took me almost an hour. I was filthy from all this cleaning. My shoes and socks were soaked and wet, and my shirt was soiled. I went and got Kassaundra so that she could go over everything. She was sitting at the bar drinking tequilla shots and talking to Mims. I interrupted the conversation and told her that I was finally done. She finished talking to Mims for another five minutes and then got up and started checking things out. Once she was done, she just grabbed her things and started turning off the lights. She never said anything to me except, "Let's go." I just stared at her, grabbed my things, and left.

Once outside, she jumped into her car and pulled out the parking lot. No bye, or anything. I just didn't understand this lady.

"This chick gets on my last nerves. I don't understand the purpose of her having me stay and clean. She could've had the crew do that," I whined.

"She did that on purpose, Carter," Mims replied.

"For what purpose?" I asked, shocked.

"Well, the other managers as well as Kassaundra have complained about how the restaurant looks after you close. They have stated the morning crew has to come clean up before they can get started," Mims advised. "She said she was going to teach you a lesson on how to close properly."

"Why wouldn't she just tell me that I wasn't doing a good job instead of trying to prove a point?" I asked.

Mims shrugged. I knew one thing; I wasn't going to be getting out of the restaurant fast any longer. I would never have to stay and clean up after the crew again. We both got into our cars and left. I was exhausted. I wasn't used to getting out of work so late.

Moving on

Travis finally got what he wanted, which was a promotion. He told me a few weeks earlier that he had an interview set up with Chris for a possible opening as a general manager at another location. He got the call the night prior that this would be his last week here and that he would be taking over his own store effective the next Monday. He was elated, but so was Kassaundra. I think she was happy that he was getting out of her restaurant. Normally, Travis was the most professional out of the group unless he was angry, but his last week at this location he decided to relax and not stress out about anything. The normal things that he would usually get upset about, he just let them go. If people were late to work or made a bad mistake, he just smiled and went about his business. It wasn't that he didn't care; he just wasn't going to let anything or anyone bother him this week.

Maria seemed bothered that he was leaving, especially since she heard it from her fellow workers and not from Travis himself. He still wasn't speaking to her since she "accidentally" spilled that water on his ex-girlfriend. She tried to start mild chitchat with him, but he kept all conversations quick with her.

There were other young ladies that worked here that liked Travis, but he would never give in to their overtures. Oftentimes, some of the female servers would flirt with him but he would ignore them. This last week was an exception, however. Travis flirted back with all the ladies who flirted with him. Most of it was all fun and games, but this girl Kenya continued nonstop with the flirtatiousness. She didn't like Maria and was jealous regarding the rumors about her and Travis fooling around. Since this was Travis's last week, any time Maria was around, Kenya would say to Travis, "Hey, since this is your last week here, we can start dating after you leave." This would get Maria hot, but it wouldn't stop Kenya.

It was funny and I thought Kenya was joking to get under Maria's skin. I knew Travis wasn't taking it seriously. At least, I thought he wasn't. On his last day working, Kassaundra had brought a cake and balloons for Travis. We gave them to him in the kitchen and he made a speech and thanked everyone for his time with them. Kenya said, "I got a gift for you too, Travis, but I put it in the office." No one thought anything of it, because several people brought him cards and little gift bags for his promotion.

Toward the end of the night, I told Travis he could get out of here and that I could close down the restaurant. I could tell he was ready to get out of here. He was cool with that because he had a meeting with our director at his new restaurant the next day. As he was still in the office gathering up his things, in walked Kenya. She had got off earlier that afternoon. She was dressed in heels and a tight-fitting skirt. She looked amazing. I was used to seeing her in her uniform and had no idea she could look this good. She asked me if Travis was still here. I told her that he was in the office. She asked if it was okay if she went back there to say goodbye to him. I told her that it was okay, and she proceeded to the office.

I got a little busy helping the bartender. I hoped Travis had not left yet because I wanted to say goodbye as well. After about twenty minutes of helping the bar, I made my rounds around the restaurant and then proceeded to the office. The door was closed, and I figured that Travis had left already. Just as I was about to insert my key in the lock, I heard moaning sounds coming from the office. This is when I realized that Travis hadn't left yet. I decided not to go in the office. I knew what was going on. Kenya was giving him his going away present. I was shocked that she was that bold.

Ten minutes later, I saw Kenya leaving the building. I went back by the office and Travis was in there still gathering his things. I looked at him and said, "Damn, I guess you got your going away present!"

He laughed and said, "Yeah, dude, I had to break her back before I left."

I said, "Good. Now your last duty here will be sanitizing this office before you leave. I'm not stepping foot in here until you wipe it down and spray in here."

He laughed, but I went and got him a bucket of sanitizer water and a towel. He joked, "You serious?"

I said, "Yes, sir!"

Travis completely wiped down the office before he left.

Jitters

Over the next couple of months that I worked with Kassaundra, we barely spoke. If she had to tell me something, she barked the orders at me as usual. I don't know what I did to get on this chick's bad side, but I couldn't take it. It was like I couldn't get anything right at all. It got to the point that I was looking at my schedule to see when she worked just so that I could work opposite shifts than her. I was able to successfully do this for a few weeks, but I think she started to take notice. One Sunday morning shift, I was scheduled to open. I was excited because I opened, Franklin was the mid-manager, and we had a visiting manager from another Blue Crab that was the closer. I had a family get together later in the evening, so this was perfect.

The only thing about this shift was when I looked on the schedule roster, I noticed that the two servers opening were the Bitch and another server named Blue! I already couldn't stand the Bitch, and Blue wasn't a bad server, but she was always late. These two servers oversaw opening up the server side of the kitchen this morning. Setting up the kitchen would mean putting ice out in all cold wells; making coffee, tea, and lemonade; setting up the salad bar, the potato bar, and dressings; and making sure back up sauces and utensils were available. They had one hour to do it. A lot of servers would complain about this. However, when I used to be a server, management would only schedule one server to do it. I had two hours to do it, by myself, and I always got done in time. The only issue with them not getting done in time was if anyone was late. And this was their problem.

Every time they were the opening servers, they would be ten to fifteen minutes late. They would wear their T-shirts while they set up so that nothing got on their nice shirts before we opened. This was no problem; most servers would do that. However, they would never be dressed when it was time to unlock the doors at 11:00 a.m. They would go running to the bathroom to put their shirts and makeup on after they had seated a table. Oftentimes, when we had guests enter the restaurant as soon as we opened, they would complain that no server stopped by their table. This was embarrassing.

Today, I didn't want this problem. I told myself that as soon as they walked in, I was going to let them know they needed to be ready at 11:00 a.m. Of course, they were both late and not in uniform. The Bitch was ten minutes late and Blue was twenty minutes late. Once they were both in the building, I approached them to advise them how this morning's setup was going to work. Of course, the Bitch had something to say. "How are we supposed to get everything set up and ready, as well as be dressed in forty minutes?"

I responded, "Well, if you all were on time, that wouldn't be a problem!"

"Yeah, okay," the Bitch responded. Blue had nothing to say.

I retorted, "If you all aren't ready to go at 11:00 a.m., then I will give your tables away to the bartender." I had threatened them with this before but had never given their tables away. The bartender always wanted tables the first hour of their shift on Sunday. You couldn't serve liquor until noon and people rarely sat at the bar early on Sunday mornings. The bartender had to be scheduled but they literally didn't have anything to do. They never minded taking those first few tables so that they could make money.

The Bitch was ready for this retort as well and said, "Yeah, I already talked to Kassaundra about that and she said that you can't give our tables away." I shook my head and walked away. I thought to myself, *Y'all better be ready.*

I came back to check on them five minutes prior to opening and they were in the kitchen having a good time. They were laughing and joking with no cares in the world. They showed absolutely no sense of urgency. "Ladies, we only have five minutes to opening. Go ahead and put your shirts on so that you will be ready." They completely ignored me. I wanted to send them home, but they were the only two servers that we had on until 11:30. I couldn't open the restaurant with no servers.

It was now 11:00 a.m. and we were open. There were already two different families waiting to be sat down. The hostess, Simone, sat the two parties and I went into the kitchen to let the servers know they were sat. Of course, they weren't dressed and had to take off to the bathrooms to put their shirts on. I guess they thought I was just playing. I went to the bartender, Sophia, and told her to take the first two tables. She was elated and ran off to take the tables. A few minutes passed by and a third table came in. The Bitch and Blue still weren't out of the restroom, so I also gave this table to Sophia.

At 11:10 a.m., the Bitch and Blue came out of the restroom. This was ten minutes after we opened and had sat our first guest.

They both went to Simone and asked which tables were first. Simone informed them both that Carter had already given the tables away. They both came charging toward the office looking for me. Of course, Blue had nothing to say but the Bitch was all talk.

"Why did you give those tables away?" she barked.

"You already know why! I told you both that if you weren't ready, I was going to give your tables away. Y'all weren't ready, so I gave them away!" I barked back.

Blue finally had something to say. "That's not fair to us. The bartender already makes eight dollars an hour plus tips. We only make two dollars and thirteen cents an hour, and now she is taking our tips. That's not fair."

I retorted, "What's not fair is having our guests wait to be serviced. You two do this every week. And every week our guests are upset while waiting to be serviced."

"Well, I'm telling Kassaundra about this. She already said that you aren't allowed to give away our tables. I'm also calling corporate on you. This some bullshit! I didn't come in to work for free," the Bitch warned.

"Well, Kassaundra is not here today, I am!" I warned back.

"No, she is coming in today. She'll be in at noon today, and I will let her know that is what you said!" she snapped.

"First of all, I don't care if you tell her and secondly, she isn't in today. Franklin is the mid," I advised.

"Oh, she will be in! She switched shifts with Franklin," the Bitch warned.

Damn, I did not know that her and Franklin had switched shifts. Not that I was concerned about this incident, I just didn't want to work with her. And how in the world did the Bitch know about this when I didn't? As if she knew what was on my mind, the Bitch smiled and stated, "Oh, you didn't even know they switched shifts. I know more about what's going on than you do. Like Maria said, are you even a real manager?"

I wanted to slap her for talking to me like this. I couldn't stand this chick. How she was even allowed to work here was beyond me. I kept my cool, though. I told her, "You keep talking to me like this, you going to find out how much of a manager I really am."

She just laughed and walked away. She told Blue, "Aw, look at our little wannabe manager trying to have some control. I can't wait for Kassaundra to come in."

I really wanted to just send her home, but I couldn't do this because I disliked her. It was now 11:30 and a couple more servers came in. This made the Bitch even more upset because now they were being sat in a rotation. She went and told the hostess to give her and Blue three tables apiece before they sat the other servers since they missed out on money. Simone came and asked me if this was okay. I told her not to listen to the Bitch and just seat them in rotation with the other servers. I don't know why the Bitch thought she was running the place.

Business started to pick up, which I was grateful for. The busier we were when Kassaundra came in, the quicker time would fly by before it was time for me to leave. It was now a few minutes before noon and I knew that Kassaundra would be walking in any minute. My stomach started hurting with the thought of her walking in the door. Just as my mind was settling on her coming in, Simone told me there was a call on the phone for a manager. I grabbed the phone and it was a customer from the day before saying they were now sick. I hated these calls. We had to collect so much information from the guest and it took too long. We couldn't blow them off and say we would call them later. We had to show empathy to the guest. Although a lot of people lie about being sick, some are telling the truth.

While I was on the phone with the customer, Kassaundra came bursting into the office. I didn't even realize that she was here yet. She was mad and tried interrupting the phone call. I motioned to the phone and mouthed to her that I was on the phone with a guest. She stood there and looked at me for a second and then walked out and closed the door. After about five more minutes she came into the office again, but I was still on the phone with the same guest. This time I never paid her any attention. I just ignored her completely. I could tell with all the huffs and puffs in the background that me ignoring her enraged her. She finally turned around and left, but not without slamming the door first. How unprofessional! I couldn't believe this chick. Five more minutes had passed and just as I was hanging the phone up with the guest, Kassaundra came charging back into the office. She was completely red with rage at this point. I thought this was ridiculous. Did she want me to hang up on the guest just to acknowledge her?

"Why did you give our tables away to the bartender?" she yelled.

"They weren't ready to take the tables and I didn't want the guests to wait," I replied.

"Haven't we talked about this before!" she continued.

"No, we never spoke about this!"

"DIDN'T ALEXANDRIA TELL YOU THAT I DIDN'T WANT YOU TO GIVE ANY TABLES AWAY TO THE BARTENDER?" Kassaundra continued, yelling.

I had to think about who Alexandria was. *Oh yeah, I forgot the*

Bitch has a name. "Yes, she told me, but I never heard this from you! And why would I listen to her? She works for me. I don't work for her," I replied.

I couldn't believe it! I was starting to shake again. I was not afraid of this lady, so why was I shaking again? I think she noticed that I had jitters because she came at me even harder. I was still sitting down in the chair and she came and stood over me. She pointed her finger in my face and said, "Listen, I am the general manager, not you. If you even think you heard that I said something, you had better follow the instructions."

When she got into my personal space and put her finger in my face, this was the moment that she fucked up! I completely lost my mind and my professionalism.

I looked at her and said, "You better get your motherfuckin' finger out of my face and back the fuck up!" I stood up and said, "Who are you talking to like this?"

She stood her ground and yelled, "I am your general manager and you had better watch your tone!"

I yelled back, "I don't care who you are, you don't speak to me like this!"

She yelled, "You better calm down, Carter!"

I yelled back, "No, you better calm down, Kassaundra!"

As I stood there staring at her, I was ready for whatever was about to happen next. I was ready for the fight and she saw that in my eyes.

She said, "So you gonna talk to a woman like this?"

I said, "Show me a woman, and I'll show her respect. The way you are acting isn't like any woman that I've ever met before."

Now, I wasn't going to hit her, but I decided that her bullying-me days were over. I wasn't scared of her and let her know! She was furious as she stared at me. She turned around and left the office. She tried to slam the door, but I grabbed the door. I was still hot and wasn't through with the conversation.

When we came out the office door, workers scurried in each direction like roaches. We were so loud as we were arguing that the workers stood by the door to get a better ear. When I saw the team members, I stopped my pursuit of Kassaundra. She walked outside the building, I guess to blow off steam. I was still so angry, but Simone ended up stopping me. She pulled me to the side and whispered, "Calm down, Mr. Sexy!" As she whispered this, her lips grazed my ear. I instantly calmed down.

I walked back into the kitchen and got me something to drink. As I calmed down, I started thinking about my job. Was I going to get fired? I didn't even care—she shouldn't have talked to me in that manner. As I was drinking water in the kitchen, I saw the Bitch out of the corner of my eye. I instantly started getting upset again. However, she didn't say a word to me. I was hoping that she did. At this point, I didn't care about my job any further. I waited for her to say one thing to me and I was going to let her have it. She never said one word to me and walked right out of the kitchen.

A few minutes went by and Kassaundra came back into the building. I was waiting on her to say something to me, but she just walked right past me. I could tell that she was still angry. I had come back down to my senses at this point. I saw her put an apron on, which meant she was going to work the kitchen. I took my apron off and ended up working the front.

We went the entire shift without speaking until it was time for me to leave. I asked her if there was anything else she needed me to do. She told me that she needed to speak with me and to meet her in the anchor. As I waited for her, the questions started again. *Here we go*, I thought. Was this it? Was she about to terminate my employment?

As I was overthinking the situation, Kassaundra walked in. She was still red with anger. She sat down and rolled her sleeves up. She was still sweating from working in the hot kitchen. The first thing she said to me was, "I could've fired you today!" She paused and looked at me as if she was trying to figure me out. Truth is, I didn't care anymore. I just looked at her and said nothing. She next said, "The only reason that I didn't was because I was completely out of line for my behavior. For that, I apologize."

I was floored! I couldn't believe that she apologized. I was going to apologize but I decided against it. This was the first time that I ever stood my ground with her and I wasn't going to relinquish that feeling. We ended up shaking hands and I left. It wasn't until I was driving home that I realized the magnitude of what had happened.

The entire time that Kassaundra and I were yelling at each other, I was not once jittery or shaking. I realized the only reason that I was shaking was because I was always trying to maintain my composure and be a professional. My instincts are when someone barks at me, I bark back. I was trying to act too professional and, in the meantime, I was losing myself. I told myself that from now on, I was going to maintain my professionalism but I wasn't going to let anyone take my kindness for weakness. This went for my coworkers and the guests.

RETRIBUTION

The cocky customer that had me reciting the mission statement to him came back to eat one evening. As soon as I saw him, I remembered him. Shame circulated through my entire body at that very moment. He saw me as well and signaled for me to come over to the table. I fake-smiled and headed toward his table. He was with a group with five other guys that seemed to be just as cocky as he was. It was apparent by their looks at me that he had boasted to them about how he schooled me in the past.

As I approached the table and said hello, he arrogantly said, "Looks as if things have gotten better around here, young man. Apparently, you must've took what I said to heart."

I gritted my teeth and tried my best to not come off across confrontational as I dryly said, "Apparently!"

He looked around at his friends like he was on stage trying to build up a moment of anticipation. He said arrogantly, "Young man, I thought it was great that you knew the company's mission statement. I was telling my friends about this and they said they would like to hear it!"

I stood there and looked at them as they all returned my gaze, expecting me to recite the mission statement. I almost laughed at them and their arrogance. I did let out a slight laugh because I knew he had to joking.

He looked at me seriously and stated, "Young man, I don't see anything funny here. I thought you learned the lessons I taught you the last time you were here, but I guess you have not."

I stood there, dumbfounded, as I looked at this man like he was out of his mind.

He continued, saying, "As a paying customer, I am demanding that you recite your company's mission statement to me and my colleagues at this very moment."

Okay, this time I did laugh, and it was a little uncontrollable. It took me some time to get myself together as the group of men sat there angrily staring at me.

Once I got myself together, the customer said, "That was quite unprofessional. Well, since you think everything is so funny, then you should laugh as you pay for this bill!"

I started laughing again as I told him that I was not going to pay for anything.

He said, "Young man, you are going to pay for our bill or I will have you fired!" They stood up to leave and I just motioned to Mims, who was standing nearby to handle this.

Mims was able to get the money and set them straight. He told me they insisted on getting our corporate number to complain on me. I didn't care. I did nothing wrong except for laugh at them for being ridiculous. If corporate wanted to give them money, it was fine, but I wasn't going to give them anything.

After moments like these, I really started to get the hang of dealing with difficult and disgruntled guests. I think I learned to never show fear under any circumstance and to exude confidence when I addressed a difficult situation. I thought I had difficult situations mastered after some time, until I met this one customer.

Once again, I was working the kitchen when I was alerted that a customer wanted to see a manager. When I finally got to the table, it was a rather large guy sitting at a booth with two other people. For the life of me, I don't know why he was sitting at a booth. You could tell he was uncomfortable. He was sitting with one leg outside the booth because his entire body couldn't fit. His knee came to the top of the table. This guy looked as if he was a professional basketball player or a heavyweight boxer. Not only was he large, but he was bulging with muscles.

When I approached the table and attempted to introduce myself, he immediately cut me off. He pushed his plate toward me and asked me loudly, "What the hell is this?"

I looked at his plate and said, "It appears to be a steak, sir!" I was trying to stay professional, but he was intent on causing a scene.

He continued, increasingly raising his voice. "No, smartass, I know it is a steak. I asked for a medium-well steak and this is a burned piece of cardboard. Every time I come here, this place can't get my steak right. What are you going to do about it?" As he said this, he pounded his fist on the table, causing the nearby tables to take notice.

I was taken aback by how loud and rude this guy had become. Furthermore, my back was to the wall. I knew I couldn't allow this behavior because I would be eaten alive by the other guests.

I stood my ground and stated, "Well, the first thing that is going to happen is that I'm not going to tolerate you talking to me like that. We are in a family restaurant and no one wants to hear that type of language. If your steak is wrong, please give me the opportunity to fix it, but talking to me in that tone won't get anything done."

After I said my piece, I stood there and waited for his response. In the corner of my eye and out of the guest's view, I saw Mims. Mims had just arrived when he noticed the guy get aggressive; he stopped and headed in my direction. I was able to smoothly hand motion to him that I had this under control.

At the same time, the guy stood up. He was larger than I expected and now I was second guessing my decision to not let Mims help me out. As the guy stood towering over me, he stated, "Young man, you are absolutely correct. Please forgive me for talking to you in that tone." He stuck out his paw and engulfed my hand as he gave me a handshake. I was startled and relieved this turned out easily.

As I walked away, Mims walked up to me and said, "You okay?" I told him that I was. He said, "Okay, great. I had your back, though." I knew he did. I was grateful to have Mims in the building.

Another altercation challenged my ability to keep it all together. We were having a manager meeting. We always had our meetings prior to opening the restaurant and attempted to be finished right before we unlocked the doors. On this particular day, our meeting ran over by about thirty minutes. It was no problem, however, because our host, Jack, was running the front. Jack would also screen any possible applicants for us. If someone walked in and asked about hiring, Jack would prescreen them for us. Also, he would do any background checks for us. Jack was a gem and we knew this.

As we were conducting our meeting, Jack came back to tell us that we had an applicant that came in who was previously employed with another Blue Crab in Tennessee. He wanted to talk to one of the managers about him joining our team. We were hurting for experienced team members so Kassaundra gave Jack the okay to call the restaurant in Tennessee to find out more information.

A few minutes later, Jack came to us laughing. He said that he spoke with the manager there, and they stated that the applicant was fired for his bad temper. They told Jack the applicant was unavailable for rehire and they would never bring him back under any circumstance. We all laughed at this guy's audacity to come in here to apply for this job, knowing that he was terminated from another Blue Crab.

Kassaundra told Jack to tell the applicant that he wasn't eligible for hire and we were going to decline. Although Jack was good at what he did, he was not a supervisor. I didn't think he should be the person to decline the applicant. It should be a manager. I told Kassaundra that I could go and talk to the guy. Jack rebutted and said, "I got this! I do this all the time." Kassaundra looked at me and said that it was okay for Jack to handle it seeing that we were almost finished with our meeting.

The meeting only lasted about five more minutes and then Kassaundra excused us. I was off for the day, so I was anxious to leave. Once she excused us for the day, I beelined to the front door to get out. I wanted to get home and enjoy the rest of my day. I completely forgot about the applicant with the bad temper who was out front. However, I got to the front just in time to see that Jack was getting slammed to the ground by the applicant. I was furious.

Before I knew it, I had run up to the guy that slammed Jack and was all in his face. He never had time to see where I came from. I acted out of reaction but was ready for the fight. I was dressed in jeans and a sweatshirt, not the typical manager attire. We weren't required to dress up for our meetings. This guy didn't know if I was a guest or an employee. I was an inch from his face, screaming at him.

"You just put your hands on this man, why don't you put your hands on me?" I yelled.

I couldn't believe the anger that was coming from me. This coward just stood there looking at me. I wanted him to make a move so I could put my hands on him, but he just stood there. After a few seconds, someone put their hand on my shoulder and pulled me back. It was Mims. I didn't know he was even at the restaurant. He was never there for lunch. When I saw him, he gave me a look of assurance that he was going to handle it.

I attempted to calm down, but then the guy must've got brave and shouted out, "You can this beat down too."

I shouted out, "Bring it!"

Mims looked at me and then at the guy and told the guy he must leave immediately. The guy looked at Mims, who would've arrested him, and then at me—I was still salivating to get to him. He thought better about it and walked out screaming obscenities toward us, but he did leave.

Mims, trying to be serious but also holding back a laugh said, "Whoa, what happened, brother?" I could hardly talk and at this time other team members started coming around as well. Kassaundra and Franklin had come up and were talking to Jack, who was still on the floor.

As Mims was talking to me, he glanced over and noticed Jack. Jack was sitting up at this point and started laughing as he told us what happened. I think he was laughing out of embarrassment. We were all concerned as we listened to him tell us what happened.

Jack stated that after he spoke to us about declining the guy the position, he went back up front to the host podium. The guy was standing there waiting impatiently for Jack, but there were also some guests waiting to be seated. Simone was also here but she was seating some other guests. Jack stated that he told the guy he would be right back while he went ahead and greeted the guests standing there waiting. It took about five minutes to get back to the guy because people kept coming in to be seated.

Once Jack got to him, the guy stated, "Look man, I got to go. When can I speak to a manager about me starting?" Jack advised him that he already spoke to the managers and they had decided to pass on hiring him. Jack stated the guy got irate and said, "So these motherfuckers can't even come tell me themselves? They send your punk ass out here to tell me that!" Jack and Simone stood there, shocked that this idiot was talking like this. Jack quickly gathered himself and told the guy it was best for him to leave. The guy just stood there looking angry, so Jack walked past him to come get us. Jack stated that as he walked past, the guy grabbed his collar from behind. Jack tried to get loose and turn around, but as they were tussling, the guy picked him up and slammed him to the ground. Jack stated that he didn't remember anything else until he saw Kassaundra and Franklin.

Mims was furious. He had no idea that all of that had occurred. He immediately went outside, followed by Kassaundra. A few minutes later, they both came back in. He looked at me and said, "Had I known that guy did all of that, I would've help you beat him down."

I asked Mims, "Man, what are you even doing up here? I never seen you up here for lunch."

I was just coming up here to drop off my security invoice to Kassaundra when I saw you about to go Mike Tyson on that guy.

Well I'm glad you were here, I stated.

Mims left and we immediately turned our attention back to Jack.

Jack ended up being okay. We bought him some lunch and told him that he could go home for the day. He insisted on staying and said he was fine, but Kassaundra insisted that he go home. We were all relieved that Jack was okay. That guy better be happy that Kassaundra didn't catch up to him.

As I gathered my things to leave, Simone came up to me and said, "Look at my soldier. I didn't know you could be so rough. That was so sexy, what you did. Thanks for having Jack's back." She hugged me and gave me a kiss on the cheek, although her lips accidentally grazed the corner of my mouth. I was turned on but decided I better get the heck out of here.

GANGSTA

After the altercation with Kassaundra, things became better between us. I think she respected me for not giving in and standing up to her. Don't get me wrong, I still thought she was gangsta and would have you come up missing if you went too far with her. I think she treated our altercation as a gang initiation. If you can take getting beat up by all the gang members without quitting or crying, then you can now become one of them. Although I did not want to be like any of them, it was cool to be accepted.

Of course, when Franklin heard about this, he was elated. As soon as he saw me, he said, "I heard you let that Big Titty Bitch have it!" I was shocked because I thought I was the only one that referred to her with that name. He knew what I was thinking and said, "What, you didn't think I knew about the nickname *B.T.?* All of us old school Blue Crabbers know this. Kassaundra even knows this is her nickname. Once she became general manager, she made everyone stop calling her that." Franklin explained that even Chris knew about it and the nickname is how Kassaundra ultimately ended up with the general manager position. I was shocked!

He told me that Chris was initially going to fire Kassaundra because there were rumors that she was drinking at work during opening hours and allowing the crew to drink on the clock as well. Franklin explained that Chris did an intense investigation and even had statements from quite a few disgruntled ex team members. Kassaundra was eventually put on administrative leave while they did the investigation.

Franklin explained that he didn't know how true this was, but during the first day of the investigation, one of the team members who wrote a statement about Kassaundra came up missing for twenty-four hours. That team member was found the next day, passed out in the hallway at a run-down apartment building down on the east side of Detroit. His face was swollen and he had cuts on his forearms and neck. When he was found, he was rushed to the hospital. After the team member was ruled stable by the doctors, the police investigated what happened. The police initially thought foul play was involved, but the team member stated that he didn't remember what happened and how he got there. The police ruled it as a possible drug deal that went wrong and closed the case.

Later on, that same day, the team member retracted his statement from the Blue Crab regarding Kassaundra and so did the other three employees as well. They all said they made up the story and it wasn't true. They all decided to end their employment effective immediately as well.

Chris was furious when the team members retracted their statements and was surprised they all quit as well. He left it alone because had they not quit; they were going to get terminated anyway for falsifying information on Kassaundra. Because he had no further information on Kassaundra, he had to bring her back on. However, at the same time an investigation was being done on Kassaundra, she was attempting to dig up dirt herself.

One of her little sneaky followers at the Blue Crab overhead Kassaundra's old GM referring to her as B.T. at one of the GM meetings that Chris was facilitating, and some of the GMs were laughing about it. Kassaundra used that little bit of information and got some statements herself. She made it sound as if she was a damsel in distress as she bluffed Chris with this information. Chris stated this was not factual and he'd never heard about it. Kassaundra provided statements to Chris and said that she made copies that she already sent to the Blue Crab's corporate office.

Although the incident was deemed circumstantial and could not be proven to be true, the allegations were enough for Kassaundra to scare the Blue Crab. She stated that she had been employed for over ten years with Blue Crab and had vast amount of experience in every department, but she had been overlooked for promotion for her own store. She stated the Blue Crab tried to terminate her under false information and that she had not been able to climb the ladder because she was a minority woman.

Everyone knew the Blue Crab wasn't being biased based off gender or race; they were being biased because she was unprofessional. However, the allegation and the suspension that turned up nothing was enough to scare the Blue Crab. Less than six months later, Kassaundra was promoted to a general manager position in Chris's area. I think he hated her for trying to play the race game. He put her in his most challenging restaurant and hoped that she would eventually quit.

Franklin added, "That's why this chick can't fire me. Every time she brings up something to Chris about me, he does nothing about it. I know he doesn't care for me either, but I know he hates Kassaundra more."

I asked Franklin if he had ever heard anything about what

really happened to the ex team member. Franklin loved to tell stories and gossip. He always began his stories with *chile*, and he would always look around like someone was going to hear him telling the story. "Chile, I know this girl that used to date him. She told me that when it first happened, he said nothing about it. He would just clam up and not say anything. About a year later, he finally confessed to her what happened and swore her to secrecy. But she was my homegirl, so she eventually told me everything when they broke up.

"He said he was just walking from the store that evening and out of nowhere a mob of guys started running toward him from both directions. He said he saw them too late to run. The guys attacked him. He tried to fight back but there were too many of them. He knew it was over when out of the corner of his eye, he saw a brick coming toward his face. He said he remembered nothing after that moment. He said when he woke up, he was blindfolded and strapped to a chair. He could hear a few guys talking and tried to act as if he was still asleep. Someone must've noticed, because one of the guys said their little snitch was finally awake.

"The room went silent after that and then the punching began. He said he could feel fists coming from everywhere as it seemed like everyone in the mob was hitting him. Someone hit him so hard that he fell over in the chair, still strapped in. He said that his head hit so hard on the floor that he forgot about the punches. As he laid on the floor, someone knelt down next to him and told him that he needed to retract his statement that he made at his job and that he needed to quit his job immediately. He told him to contact his other little buddies and tell them the same thing. This person whispered to him that he knew where he lived and if the statement wasn't retracted in twenty-four hours, they would find him and the others and it would be worse next time.

"He shook his head that he understood and then the chair he was in was yanked back up. Someone cut the rope that had him bound and walked him out the room. They said he was getting released and then someone pushed him down a flight of stairs still blindfolded. He heard a group of guys laughing before he passed out again. When he awoke, he was in an ambulance. His ex said he knew this was because of Kassaundra, but he was going to leave it alone."

I looked at Franklin with disbelief. I said, "That story seems a little fishy. All of that over a restaurant job?"

Franklin said, "At first, I didn't believe it either, but something does seem to be a little off with Kassaundra. That bitch is gangsta."

No Longer a Pushover

Even though the story seemed unbelievable, I wasn't going to chance it. I was glad that I stood up to Kassaundra, but I wasn't going to test her. Being bound and blindfolded while being punched didn't seem appealing to me. However, after standing up to Kassaundra, I never let a guest run over me again. Now, it never stopped a guest from trying me, but I quickly let them know that it was going to work in their favor. I never got rude or unprofessional unlike Franklin, but I always stayed composed and professional if I had to reprimand a guest or ask them to leave. Some guests tested my professionalism, but in the end, I always kept it together.

As mentioned earlier, the relationship between me and Kassaundra became better as I continued to prove myself. She would often send me to tables to defuse a situation because I was the manager who was most likely to maintain professionalism and keep it together. It was tough to keep it together at this location because often times the guests had no restaurant etiquette and thought what they were doing was not a problem.

The first time Kassuandra sent me to a table after our altercation was a little challenging. It was a group of twelve people eating. It was later in the night, but we still had a fair number of tables dining with us. This group of twelve was cursing so loud the entire restaurant could hear them.

I went to the table and introduced myself to the group. They looked irritated that I interrupted them. I politely stated that while we are elated to have them dining in with us, we were a family restaurant with children dining in. I asked them if they could tone it down a little. Of course, they weren't happy with me asking them to tone it down. One of the guys at the table stated they weren't going to settle down and if they were spending their money with us, then they could act any way they wanted to. I tried to stay calm as I felt my temper rising. I once again politely asked if they could tone it down just a little. The same guy, along with others at the table, said they weren't going to quiet down at all. Fortunately, they hadn't received their food yet. I told them they could all leave then.

I was so sick of people taking my kindness for weakness that I formed a quick trigger. I was not about the nonsense. Now that I asked them to leave, they wanted to be nice and try to make a deal. My mind was made up and there was no turning back. When they noticed I was serious, they wanted to curse and fuss at me. I just walked away, grabbed Mims, and let him handle it. Once Mims got involved, they were out the building in about three minutes.

After they left, I went around and apologized to the remaining guests that were nearby. What surprised me was the remaining guests were upset with me for kicking them out. They stated the group was just having fun and so what if they were cursing. Somebody said, "Dude, we in the hood, what you expect!" I stopped talking to the rest of the tables because I thought they were ridiculous. That was always the answer: "We in the hood."

So, are we supposed to adapt to hood mentality? No, I'm about raising the mentality, not adapting.

Another occasion, I was working in the kitchen and a server walked in and stated there was a customer standing outside the kitchen asking to speak to a manager. As soon as I came out the kitchen, there was a man standing with his arms folded, looking angry. I came toward him and in an angry tone, he growled, "Are you the manager?"

I politely said that I was. At this exact time, some other customers came walking down the aisle trying to get past us. To be courteous, I stepped back closer to the wall so that they could squeeze by. I guess this fool of a customer thought when I stepped back against the wall that I was frightened by his stature. He stepped up so close to me and put his finger in my face. I was shocked, not nervous by his behavior.

For the first time with a guest, I didn't maintain my professionalism. I looked up at him and growled at him this time as I said, "You better step back off me and get your damn finger out of my face." I think he was just as shocked as I was that I lost my composure. I was ready for the fight, but I don't think he was.

He was now the polite one as he said, "Whoa, young man, settle down. I was just upset about my food, but I'm not trying to fight about it."

"Well, why were you all in my face then?" I questioned. Now this idiot was trying to be polite. I was able to find out what the problem was and resolve it without any further incidents with him.

Customers have to be careful how they treat workers. We are here to service their needs, but not take crap from them! I turned a corner in my management journey and grew up! I was proud of myself.

Thank you for reading *The First Course*, the second installment of the Restaurant Diaries. If you enjoyed this book, please help spread the word by leaving an onine review. Thank you!

Stayed tuned for the next installment of the Restaurant Diaries, *Happy Hour*, to find out what happens next during Carter's journey in the restaurant world.

The following excerpt is a preview of the first chapter of *Happy Hour*. Is this a teaser of things to come in Carter's management journey? Who knows?

HAPPY HOUR

CAN I TASTE IT?

As I continued to become more familiar with the crew, I found out that some of them were pretty cool. We had some pretty women working here as well and they were very flirtatious. I made up my mind that I would not get caught up with any of them. I did not want those problems. The Blue Crab didn't allow this anyway. That's why I was surprised that my fellow manager, Travis, had sex with Kenya on his last day. I already was trying my best to stay away from Simone and her enticing ways.

Unfortunately, I ended up getting myself suckered into a situation. I didn't plan on getting myself in a situation. It just happened. I remember thinking, "How did I get myself in this predicament?"

When I first started working there, this Malorie chick couldn't stand me. Every time I would attempt talking to her or check her in (a pre-shift talks to servers), she always seemed to have an attitude. She was borderline rude to me every time I would speak to her. I remember sitting her down to talk to her regarding her near-insubordinate attitude to me. I even asked her was their anything that she needed from me to ensure that we had a positive working environment when we were working together. She told me there was nothing that I could do, and she walked away from me. Now here I was trying to be professional and courteous, but when she walked away from me, I just wanted to fire her on the spot.

However, working for a corporate restaurant, we had to make sure we followed all rules and standards regarding progressive discipline. I could see our corporate office reaction: "So you fired her because of what?" My response: "Because I don't like her!" This would never work. Furthermore, I may have found myself getting fired for this.

* * *

Anyhow, as time passed by, I noticed that she would always be staring at me. I thought nothing of it at first, but I noticed it often. People at work started mentioning to me that she had a crush on me. I was like no way! But after time and repeated staring, I started thinking that maybe she did! Great, a psycho girl had a crush on me!

Unexpectedly, she would start hanging around the manager's office when I was closing at night. I would completely ignore her as I continued my work. After a time, she started talking to me more and more. After a couple of weeks of mild chitchat, she asked me could I take her home because her ride didn't come yet. I told her that I couldn't take her home and that it was against company policy for a manager to take an employee home. Although this policy was true, I had taken several people home before in the past. She wouldn't give up and every couple of weeks, she would ask if I could take her home. My response was always the same. Nope, nope, and nope!

After this didn't work, she started hugging me every night before she would leave. The hug went from a friendly hug to an awkwardly long, lingering hug. I would literally have my hands to my sides, and she would still be hugging me for about ten seconds. I would be like, "Umm, could you let me go?" Finally, this is how she tricked me into taking her home.

One day as I was leaving work, it was raining hard. It had been raining for hours. It was not only raining but it was cold and windy outside. I could think of nothing more but to hurry up and get home. As I was walking outside, there was Malorie standing under the awning! She begged me to take her home and was again stating that her ride had not come, and she didn't want to be stuck in this rain as she waited for the bus at the bus stop. Regrettably, I finally gave in and said yes. I was irritated at this point, but I truly didn't want to see the young lady get stuck outside in the rain.

When she got into my car, I did let her have it, stating to her this was the first and last time that I would ever take her home and to not ask me anymore. She was nice and apologetic, so at this point I felt no reason to rant any further. I just turned the radio up and started to drive. I would have to turn the music down from time to time to get further directions from her, but I was not inter-ested in any small talk with her. As we pulled up to her house, she asked me if she could talk to me for just a few minutes. I said that I really didn't want to talk and that I was really tired and just wanted to go home. She begged me to talk to her for a quick minute. As I pulled into her driveway, agitated, I said, "Sure, what's up?"

She spilled her feelings out to me.

"Carter, I like you. You are a very nice person and I just enjoy being around you even though it is at work."

I just sat there awkwardly, listening.

"Can we spend time together outside of work?" she begged.

I again stated to her that this would not be an option for me. I gave her the company line regarding fraternization and the fact that I was her manager.

"No one has to know, and I will keep very quiet about it!"

I again said no, and I was not interested in putting my job on the line.

"Question for you," I said. "Why were you so mean and rude to me when I first started to work here?"

"Carter, I knew right away that I was attracted to you. From the first moment I met you I had feelings for you and wasn't sure how you would react to that. I didn't know if you had a girlfriend or if I even had a chance to date you since I knew about the fraternization policy. So, for me, the best thing for my mindset was to stay away from you. After a time, however, I realized that I couldn't stay mean to you because my feelings for you were too strong," Malorie confessed.

She even told me that she almost got into a fight with the Bitch. She said that every time the Bitch said anything bad about me or gave me a hard time, she would be upset.

"Carter, please reconsider us hanging out. I am a nice person and I really care for you."

For the last time, I said no and that I would not cross that line.

She said, "Okay, then I can respect that, but I just have one last question for you."

I said, "Sure, what is it?"

She said, "Can I taste it?"

I said, "Taste what?"

As she was looking down directly into my lap, she pointed to my crotch and said, "Can I taste that?"

TO BE CONTINUED ...

QUESTIONS

1. What happened with Malorie and Carter?
2. Will Carter become victim number four in Simone's love conquest?
3. Franklin mentioned that something was off with Kassaundra. What do you think it was?
4. Will Franklin remain a manager with the Blue Crab?
5. Will Carter's jitters come back, or does he have that conquered?
6. What characters, if any, do you think will appear in the next installment?
7. Since Travis is gone, who will become the next manager? Is it someone that is already working there?
8. Will anyone ever be able to control Maria?
9. Were you fooled about the executive office, or did you realize that A.J. was stringing Carter on?
10. What was your favorite chapter/story and why?